The Big Farm
in Old Sodus

by
Michael Leonard Jewell

To my dear Heavenly Father—
what a privilege it is to know You
through faith in Your Son, Jesus Christ.

To "Uncle Jerry" Darling of the Rural Bible Mission,
who preached the gospel at Chadwick School in Sodus Township,
bringing this young boy under conviction,
showing him his need of the Savior.

To Printis Jewell, my great-great-grandfather,
a pioneer who came to Sodus in 1860 from Erie County, New York.

Table of Contents

Years Ago · 1
Jebediah · 3
That Old Hollow · 11
A Snowy Surprise · 19
As Long As You Are Happy · 28
Like Wildfire · 31
The Waiting · 41
The New Resident · 45
The Treasures of Our Lives · 57
Keeping It Going · 69
Karl · 74
Lien Confides in an Old Friend · 84
Setting Matters Straight · 88
Lien Takes Matters into Her Own Hands · 101
Mrs. Davison Comes to the Rescue · 110
Beth · 115
Fourth of July Picnic · 121
Jeb Goes Another Round · 130
Surprises Come in Threes · 134
Sam Wants to Know · 146
The Harvest Supper · 155
Thanksgiving in the Windy City · 165
A Wonderful Gift · 181
A Sweet Interlude · 188
Christmas On the Big Farm · 197
Surely Unexpected · 202

Years Ago . . .

It was an early March evening in Sodus Township, and a soft, misty rain had fallen all day on the big farm in Hipps Hollow. A flock of newly arrived robins, chanting their evening carols in the hazelnut trees next to the small cottage by the barn, huddled together to stay warm. In one of the cottage's two rooms lay a young, handsome woman with auburn hair. The roughly hewn wooden bed upon which she rested was held solidly together by hand-whittled wooden pegs, its thin, unyielding mattress supported only by a lattice of woven hemp rope.

The woman was exhausted, and heavy moisture ran down her colorless face as she labored for every breath. Her vigilant young husband, after carefully stoking the fire, patted her face with a damp cloth. He had gone several times to the big farmhouse for help, but no one was home. He finally resolved that he must see his wife through this alone.

As he held her cold hand in his, his nervous attention was drawn across the room to a small woven basket upon their only table. Its outline was softly illuminated by the yellow light that shone through the isinglass of the cast-iron stove. Inside the basket, wrapped in a blue flannel blanket, lay the lifeless body of their newborn son.

"Jebediah, are you there? Jebediah?"

The husband, suddenly brought back to reality by the squeeze of his wife's hand and the urgency of her voice, turned to look into her full brown eyes.

"I'm here, Abi! Don't talk, now!"

"Oh, Jeb—our boy, our poor boy! Let me hold him one more time."

The young man let his hand slip from his wife's hand, and he crossed the floor and tenderly cradled the lifeless form in his arms. Pulling the covers back, he laid the baby beside his wife and tucked her arm securely around him. She leaned her face close to the tiny ball of flesh, kissed the coolness of the death dew that had settled upon his forehead, and wept.

Perhaps an hour or more passed as the rain fell and the darkness outside worried at the windows and doors. Jebediah held Abi and their son until he was lulled into sleep. The sound of her labored breathing woke him with a start, and he gripped her hand, watching her peaceful face as her breaths became fewer and shallower. Finally, her last reach for a mouthful of air marked the departing of her spirit as it passed upward on its way to join that of her little boy in heaven.

Jebediah nestled his face against those precious faces and wept until he could weep no more.

One
Jebediah

The kitchen blazed with light one early December morning as Sam sat down to coffee. The wind raged blustery and cold, and he was not looking forward to leaving the warmth of the woodstove to feed and milk the cows. Mary and Grandma Andrews were making breakfast, and as the pan of hot buttermilk biscuits came out of the oven, Sam grabbed one and tossed it to Jeb as he blew through the kitchen door from the cold outside.

Jeb, the hired man, stopped to warm his hands over the stove. Bits of snow fell from his coat and grizzled beard, sizzling to steam against the black cast-iron that was now glowing red around the chimney.

"Turrable cold this mornin', Miss Marion! Turrable cold! Hope the milk don't freeze," he said, munching on the steaming hot biscuit.

"Haven't you any warmer gloves than those moth-eaten things? I declare, Jeb Sanders, I haven't seen so many bare fingers sticking through a pair of gloves since the Great Depression," Grandma Andrews scolded.

"Sam's got several new pairs you can have, Jeb. There's no reason for you to go around like that," Mary said kindly. "I'll get them for you."

"Thankee much, Miss Mary!" Jeb said with his usual contriteness.

Jeb was less than domestically diligent, and Mary constantly tried to make sure that he had enough to eat and proper clothes to wear. As he sprinkled pepper on his hot biscuits and gravy, Sam began to discuss the day's activities with him.

"The dairy called, Jeb. The milk run is late this morning due to the weather. Take your time and get plenty warm."

"Yessir, Sam," he said. "That I will."

With a sudden clatter, Amberley and Brenda came rushing down the stairs to the breakfast table as if they were in a race. They were the daughters of Sam and Mary Bridges and both in their senior year of high school. Brenda was adopted, but no one seemed aware of that anymore. She had once been a rough-and-tumble bully on the playground at school but now had become a lady, thoughtful and reserved. Her shiny black hair and delicate brown skin betrayed her Native American ancestry.

Amberley, who had been shorter than Brenda as a young girl, was now just as tall. Her flaming red hair had grown darker, and with her freckled cheeks, she was very pretty—something she would not allow herself to believe.

Both girls seemed to be transforming into graceful young women overnight.

"Girls!" Mary exclaimed with some irritation. "Are you trying to give us all heart attacks?"

"Sorry, Ma," Brenda said. "It's chilly upstairs, and we wanted to get in by the stove."

"And I could smell the sausage frying," Amberley said, laughing.

"Well, I wish you girls would show the same enthusiasm going up the stairs to bed. Where's Lien?" Mary asked, attempting to hide a smile.

"She's coming, Ma," Amberley said, reaching for a plate and utensils.

The old farm was beginning to come alive again since the Bridges family had moved there from the village of Sodus. It had belonged to Grandma Andrews for many years until she signed over the deed to Sam and Mary, her beloved son-in-law and daughter. It was now her desire to live on the old farm quietly in the background and let them run things.

Under Sam and Mary's watch, the egg-and-dairy business was becoming quite respectable, and Sam had plenty of new ideas for the farm's future. With the many maple trees in the hollow, Sam envisioned starting a syrup operation in a year or two. With all of the deep, cold springs on the land, he could also grow watercress, an edible aquatic plant enjoyed in salads and sandwiches. He might also grow cranberries and Christmas trees or start a catfish farm. Sam believed the successful farmer of the future would have to practice diversity in his operations and not count on one or two things.

But these were bold ideas and would take younger, stronger hands to make them happen. Jeb's appearance reminded him of this.

"Mary, I think it's time to consider hiring another hand for the farm," Sam announced, spooning the steaming grits into a bowl. "Jeb and I are almost to the point that we can't keep up with it. With some of the things we want to do later on, we certainly will be at a disadvantage."

"I agree, Sam—it seems you and Jeb are working later and later every day. By next summer's end, you'll both be worn to a frazzle," Mary said as she sat down in her place.

"I think some younger blood is what this farm needs. Two old warhorses like Jeb and me can only do so much. What do you think, Mom?" Sam asked, looking over at Grandma Andrews, who was buttering a slice of toast.

"Are you asking for *my* advice? I told you kids when I gave you this place that I wasn't going to interfere."

"Mom?" Sam said, reaching across the table and putting his hand on hers. "That was your idea, not mine. I have always valued your input, and I really want to know what it was like in those days when Dad ran this place and it was busy as a beehive. Who could be more qualified than you to give me the benefit of that wisdom?"

Grandma Andrews smiled and blushed. "Okay, let me think on it for a while."

Jeb sat quietly, listening intently to their conversation. His hand had begun to shake, and twice he dropped his fork. No one seemed to notice as he made an effort to steady himself.

"Good morning, all!" Lien said cheerfully as she came down the stairs to breakfast.

Lien, their adopted Vietnamese daughter, was almost thirteen years old now and had started the eighth grade that September. It was obvious that unless she had an unexpected spurt of growth, she would never be tall like her sisters. Mary had cut her glossy black hair into a pageboy style because it was so thick and straight. This, with her dainty features, gave her a sweet look that matched her personality.

Lien kissed her father on the cheek and whispered "Good morning!" to him in Vietnamese. Sam smiled. "And good morning to you, sweetie," he replied in kind. Sam had learned to speak the language fluently while serving with the Special Forces in Vietnam. He and Lien often spoke to each other in her native tongue. It was a little bond between them, and they enjoyed it. Mary shook her head and smiled at the exchange.

* * *

Later that afternoon, Sam came through the back door with a pail of fresh milk, the bitter wind blowing hard behind him. Mary quickly poured him a cup of hot coffee and kissed him tenderly on the cheek.

"Sit down and get warm, dear. Supper won't be ready for another hour or so."

"The stock are secure for now, and except for the five-o'clock milking, I think we'll call it a day. It's just too cold," Sam said, rubbing his hands over the stove. "Jeb will work himself sick if I don't stop him. Several times today I've had to tell him to slow down and take a break." He sighed. "Ever since I took over the farm, he feels he must keep proving himself to me."

The next day was more of the same—the second day of a two-day snowstorm. After the supper dishes were cleared that evening, Jeb followed Sam out to secure the stock against the wind and bitter cold. The snow was blowing hard, making it difficult to see the narrow path to the barn.

"Even a gas lantern with double mantles doesn't cut through this stuff very well, Jeb."

"Well, Sam," Jeb shouted through the shrieking wind, "if ya gets lost and miss the barn, jus' keep walkin' til ya get to the woods and then stop. I'll find ya!" Sam smiled in the howling snow—Jeb's words were strangely comforting.

The next morning, Sam and Jeb sat at the kitchen table. The wind had subsided some, but it was still bitter cold. The kitchen windows facing northward were completely covered with frost except for a few places Sam had scraped off to look outside. Sam took a drink from his cup and scrutinized Jeb, who was struggling to butter a hot corn muffin with his rough hands. They were scarred and marked from many years of hard work, and he was missing a finger on his right hand. Jeb was in his sixties but could easily pass for an older man. He had a wizened face, and his hair and beard were salt-and-pepper gray. He had faithfully worked for the Andrews family for many years, and his wife and only child were buried in the little family cemetery on the orchard hill. He lived his lonely day-to-day existence in the small wooden cottage near the barn with never a word of complaint.

"How you gettin' along, Jeb?" Sam asked, looking hard at his hired man.

Jeb lifted his head in surprise, wiping crumbs from the corner of his mouth. "I'm doin' okay, Sam."

Sam leaned forward in his chair. "I mean, how do you *feel?* When's the last time you saw a doctor or dentist?"

Jeb wrinkled his forehead apprehensively. "Well, I gits tired sooner than I used ta, and I ain't seen no doctor in my whole life. I seen a dentist once, years back, when I got my store-bought teeth."

"Jeb, I'm going to have Mary make a doctor's appointment for you, for a checkup. Then we are going to send you to the dentist—just for good measure—to see what kind of shape you are in."

Michael Leonard Jewell

"But Sam, I feels good enough to work, and my teeth don't hurt none."

"Just humor me, Jeb. I want to make sure you're fit, that's all."

Two

That Old Hollow

It was late in the evening of the following day, and the supper dishes had been cleared. Lien sat at the kitchen table doing her homework, a habit she had practiced since she was a little girl. Sam came through the back door, stamping the snow from his boots on the rug. Lien watched him hang up his coat and hurried to sweep up the snow that had scattered over the floor before it melted into a puddle.

"Thanks, sweetie," he said with a wink and a smile.

"Daddy? Can we hitch up Gray and go for a sleigh ride on Saturday—just you and me? I've heard that a big flock of wild turkeys has been seen along the woods across the road."

Sam put his head back and laughed out loud at how quickly Lien could change gears. "Well, where did that come from?" he asked, pouring himself a cup of coffee from the pot on the stove and snatching an oatmeal cookie from a plate on the counter. "Yes, I guess we can, if the weather holds and your mother and the farm can spare us for a while."

"I think it would be good for you both," said Mary, who had just walked into the kitchen, "but I hope you're not thinking of going back to that old hollow."

The warning tenor could be heard in Mary's voice. "That old hollow" was Hipps Hollow, the deep, dark woods that surrounded the big farm and provided the southern border of Sodus Township along the St. Joseph River. It had once been the storybook place of wonder and imagination Mary had known as a little girl, and the long-time home of Andy and Sarah Buckles, the poor black couple who had befriended her as a child and had since moved away. But now, the circumstances surrounding the hollow—the deaths of Lien's parents, Mary's own near-fatal accident with a pickup truck several Christmases ago, and more recently, Brenda's kidnapping—made it a dark, unsavory place to be shunned. It wasn't the hollow's fault, Mary knew that, but it seemed that bad people and bad things had intruded into the sweet, idyllic world of her childhood. Mary wondered if she would ever be able to rise above her feelings regarding Hipps Hollow, and she had to admit to herself that she had become afraid of it.

"I'm sorry, Sam," Mary said finally, breaking the long moment of silence. "I have some things that I have to work through. Don't let me rain on your parade."

"Well, Lien, I guess it's a date," Sam said, looking hard at his wife and wishing that he could read her thoughts.

The Big Farm in Old Sodus

* * *

Early the next Saturday morning, after a good breakfast of fried cornmeal mush, crispy side pork, biscuits, and eggs, Sam and Lien set out across the wide, open field east of Hillandale Road toward the woods. Gray, their old faithful horse, pulled the sleigh effortlessly along the furrows of the harvested cornfield that lay beneath the snow. The sleigh bells sounded in rhythm with every shake of leather and drop of hoof.

"Daddy, where was the place?" Lien asked softly.

He looked down momentarily, letting the horse lead. "The place? I don't understand, sweetie."

Lien leaned her head against her father's arm.

Then he understood. His daughter was referring to the rough little hut in Hipps Hollow that had caught fire several years before, taking the lives of her Vietnamese parents. He had always known she would have to go back there someday. But now?

Gently, he asked, "Honey, are you sure you want to go there?"

"Yes . . . now is the time."

"Okay," Sam muttered, and then, pulling the reins hard to the right, he set out for the hollow. The sleigh made its way along the rutted and sometimes steep narrow road until it came to a stop near Love Creek by a grove of pines. It had been snowing all morning, and the snow was becoming heavier now. The only sound was its steady whispering as it filtered down through the trees.

"There, sweetie. The place was over there," Sam said, pointing to a pile of dead pine branches jutting up out of the deep snow. Even though the air was cold and crisp, his mind wandered back to that rainy night five years ago and the things he had witnessed. He could almost smell the hot, oily smoke of scorched pine in the air.

Lien jumped down and walked a few steps through the thick snow. The "place" was unremarkable, and she remembered so little of that night. Her parents had thrown her clear of the blazing pines just before they perished, leaving her to wander aimlessly in the cold, wet darkness of the hollow. The snow-covered grove little resembled the picture she held in her mind, but it did represent her parents' last act of love, and she wanted to do something special as a memorial. She stood motionless. She did not know what to do.

Almost as if Sam could read her mind, he spoke. "Honey, I have an idea. How about as soon as the weather permits, I come back here and clean this up? Then we can plant a garden here. You can make it as nice as you want. I saw a lot of beautiful gardens in Saigon, and I have a few ideas. This isn't the tropics, but I think we can make it very nice."

Her heart became lighter as Lien turned back to the

sleigh. "Oh, Daddy, could we? That would be so wonderful! Then can we keep it as a garden for always?"

"If I have anything to say about it we can."

Sam reached out to Lien and helped her into the sleigh. She quickly pulled the heavy blanket up to her neck and laid her head against Sam's arm, snuggling up close to him as the heavy snow fell and settled on her eyelashes. Sam spoke gently. "Go ahead and cry if you want. There is no shame to cry about this."

Lien closed her eyes, her arm wrapped around her father's. "No, Daddy. I don't think they would want me to cry anymore."

* * *

After lunch on the following Monday, Jeb put on his heavy coat and scarf and buckled up his rubber boots. He rose from the three-legged wooden stool by the kitchen door but just as quickly sat back down, wincing with pain. His knees felt like they were on fire as he carefully turned his head to see if anyone in the kitchen had noticed. Mary and Grandma Andrews were busy carrying dishes to the sink, and both their backs were turned. Relieved, Jeb stood up again, holding his breath to mask the pain, and slipped through the back door to continue his chores. As he hobbled out toward the toolshed, he suddenly decided to make a detour to the big barn.

In the back corner was a makeshift office, well insulated and heated. Once inside, Jeb closed the door, shutting out the sounds of the howling wind. He flipped on the light switch and turned down his lantern, which he hung on a bent nail on the wall. Assuring himself that he was quite alone, he sat down on the old couch, which was in reality an old bench seat from a pickup truck. He rubbed his knees and grimaced in an attempt to stave off the pain of rheumatism that shot through his legs like electricity. Salty drops of moisture formed at the corners of his eyes in response.

Just then, Jeb heard the door open behind him, and he turned to look. It was Sam.

"Jeb, what's going on here?" Sam said finally after a few moments of silence.

Jeb hung his head, not knowing what to say. Sam took off his hat, slapping it several times across his own leg, and then sat down next to him. "Is it that bad, Jeb?"

"Ah can still do muh job, Sam. I'll work harder. Please don't get rid of me." Jeb's body began to tremble. "I don't want ta beg ya, but I gots no place to go!"

Sam reached out and gripped Jeb's hand to calm him down. "Now, no one is going to get rid of anybody, Jeb. Why didn't you tell us you were hurting so?"

Jeb looked up at Sam, the bright ceiling light dancing in his worried eyes. "Some nights, my bones hurt so bad that I cries out in pain and can't sleep," he said, rubbing his knees furiously. "I'ze 'shamed and 'fraid to tell Miss Marion, 'cause she might run me off iff'n I can't work no more."

Sam tightened his jaw and shook his head, deeply moved by Jeb's pathetic words and tears. He had been blind to the fact that his faithful hired man had been living a life of insecurity and worry, believing that at any moment he might be discharged if he were physically unable to do his work. No wonder Sam's suggestion that he see a doctor had so troubled him!

"Jeb, I've seen you limping for a long time, but I had no idea it was this bad. You should have told us." Sam paused. "But maybe we just failed to notice and to let you know just how much we think of you and how much you mean to us." He put his arm around Jeb's bony shoulder. The old man clasped his hands together, not sure of what would happen next.

"Jeb? Mary and I have been discussing it for some time and were keeping it as a surprise for Christmas, but I see it's something we should have done a long time ago. We're going to move you into the spare bedroom off the kitchen. It's large and has its own bathroom. You will be comfortable there, and the ladies can dote over you." Sam straightened his broad shoulders, every inch the boss. "As of this very moment you are officially retired, and you will still get your full pay every week as a pension. You are family here, and we want you to be in the house with the rest of us."

Jeb was stunned. He sat quietly next to Sam on the old car seat, looking terribly small, and then he broke down and began to weep pitifully. "Nobody's ever been good to ol' Jeb like you," he finally blurted out through his tears.

"Let's go, Jeb," Sam said, helping Jeb to his feet. "You're going to the doctor right now. We're going to find out what's ailing you and get you some medicine for those tired old bones."

Three
A Snowy Surprise

 Christmas was less than three weeks away, and Brenda had been knitting a long blue scarf for Joe Schenkle, her longtime schoolmate and friend. He always seemed to like the homemade things she made for him, but this time, her heart wasn't in it. She had worked on the scarf off and on for weeks, and finally one day, in frustration and fury, she stuffed it into one of her clothing drawers—yarn, needles, and all!

 Things had grown cold between Brenda and Joe since that day many months ago when she'd confided in him—almost gloatingly—about her scholarship. Mrs. Holloway, the wealthy widow from King's Landing, had presented Brenda and her sisters with a generous gift that would allow them to go to school anywhere they wanted for as long as they wanted. Joe had evidently been in love with her but had always considered her out of his reach. The news of the scholarship only signaled her journey further up the ladder away from him, scholastically and socially. She rarely saw him anymore outside of school, and then, only a few cordial words were spoken.

On a snowy Friday evening after a long, tedious week of school, Brenda dressed warmly and announced that she was going for a walk alone. During the last several months, especially since she and Joe had gone their separate ways, Brenda had started taking short walks after supper, sometimes with Lien or Amberley but most times alone. She had come to look forward to her constitutional every night, as walking gave her a chance to unwind and reflect.

"Don't stay out too late, dear, and don't go too far," Mary said. "I don't want you to get lost in all this snow." Mary looked at her daughter as she wrapped her scarf around her neck, noting the way Brenda moved like someone deep in thought. It pained her to see Brenda brooding over her problems at such a young age.

Sam, who was seated in his big chair, looked over his paper at Brenda with a smile but said nothing.

"I will go with you, Brenda," Lien said, looking up from her book.

"No, sweetie, but thank you. I want to be alone tonight."

Amberley was finishing up the supper dishes and paused to make eye contact with Brenda as she opened the kitchen door. She knew that Brenda was thinking about Joe, but she didn't know what to say or how to help. Amberley had her own ideas on the matter and believed that her sister had strung Joe along. When he wearied of what he considered an impossible courtship, he'd decided to let Brenda go. Brenda had been ruing the day ever since.

The falling snow and windless night muffled all sounds so that Brenda could barely hear her own footsteps. She could see the soft brightness in the northwestern sky over Lake Michigan from the twin cities of Benton Harbor and St. Joseph. As her eyes adjusted to the night, the thickening snow cover took on a glow, and she could faintly see across the big fields east of Hillandale Road. It was a dream world, and Brenda felt invisible and alone.

As Brenda walked toward the woods at the far end of the field, her heart ached as she thought about Joe. He was so tall and handsome, and she felt safe when she was with him. She thought about how he would tease her and the way he smiled when she fussed at him about different things. He never took her minor scoldings too seriously, and Brenda needed that edge of his grace. She was surprised at herself as she realized the pent-up feelings she had for him. It made all of the petty disagreements and differences of the past seem so unimportant.

As she scuffed along in the gradually accumulating snow, she watched a herd of deer near the edge of the woods that did not seem to be threatened by her approach. Suddenly, a big buck stuck his nose into the air and snorted. Then, as one, the whole herd turned and bounded off into the snowy forest. Had she frightened them, or had something else startled them? Perhaps it was a pack of coyotes, a bobcat, or maybe one of the cougars that had been sighted in Berrien County over the years. Brenda stood still in the feathery world of snow, suddenly feeling vulnerable.

I'd better go back, she thought and turned to walk toward the farm. As she neared Hillandale Road, she thought she could hear the muffled sound of sleigh bells in the distance. The sound became louder and louder, and then she saw a small sleigh being pulled by a single horse, rising in an instant over the breast of the hill on Hipps Hollow Road. The image was gray in the steadily falling snow, like a smear of ashes against muslin cloth, almost indiscernible except for the light from the gasoline lantern that hung from a hook at its side.

"Whoa, Gypsy," the driver said, stopping just in front of Brenda.

It was Joe Schenkle, dressed in his thick, warm coat and hat with several heavy woolen blankets across his lap. Tied to the back of the sleigh was a freshly cut Christmas tree, every bit of seven feet long.

After a pause of silence and surprise, Brenda spoke.

"Uh, hi!" she said nervously, with a slight wave of her hand.

"You look mighty cold, girl," Joe said, peeking through the woolen scarf wrapped around his face. "Would you like to go for a ride and get warm?"

Brenda didn't hesitate. She quickly slipped under the

The Big Farm in Old Sodus

warm blankets beside him.

Joe whistled, and Gypsy turned and headed toward the dark outline of the snowy woods in the distance. The bells shook and chirped in rhythm as the faithful horse pulled the sleigh along the tree line and then made a circle to return to the big house in the distance. Brenda was going to ask about the tree strapped to the sleigh, but Joe beat her to it.

"I spoke to your pa earlier today, an' he said you folks hadn't cut your tree yet. I told him that I had some nice ones in our woods and I would be obliged to bring one over — sort of a gift from the Schenkle bunch to you all."

"That was mighty nice of you, Joe. And I thank you for the trouble of coming all this way in a sleigh on such a snowy evening," Brenda said, smiling.

"Well, it's Christmastime, and I thought it would be nice. Have you ever driven a sleigh?"

"No," Brenda said, as Joe handed her the reins, "but I'm willing to give it a try." She chuckled a little, remembering how nervous she had been the first time she touched Gray's nose and fed him a sugar cube. But she had learned to like horses, and they seemed to like her.

"Okay, just hold the reins firmly and try not to jerk 'em. Keep steady pressure. Gypsy knows what she's doin' and is as gentle as a mouse."

Brenda started to laugh as the sleigh glided with ease over the snow-covered fields.

"Did I say somethin' funny?" Joe asked.

Brenda chuckled again. "Gentle as a mouse! I've never thought of a mouse as being gentle."

"I guess I shouldn't tell you about the little brown field mouse with the white belly that I kept as a pet when I was a little boy," Joe said with a grin.

"Oh no, Joe! You didn't!"

"I sure did. I kept him in a homemade cage in my room, and he made a mighty fine pet too, until he slipped through the bars one night. I think the cat got him."

Brenda laughed until she cried. Her heart felt light for the first time in many months. She had missed being with Joe. He made her laugh, and that made her happy.

Soon Joe pulled the sleigh into the yard and stopped it near the back door. Brenda hated to get out from under the warm blankets, and she suddenly realized that she had wrapped her arm around Joe's. He didn't seem to mind—or notice, for that matter—as he climbed out of the sleigh to untie the tree. Joe dragged the tall pine tree up onto the porch and struck the trunk several times against the deck to shake off the powdery snow.

The porch light came on, and the back door opened.

"What's all this?" Amberley said with a smile, and then she squealed with delight when she saw the tree. "Lien, come see the Christmas tree!"

Joe greeted everyone as he dragged the fragrant tree through the kitchen to the large living room.

"Hello, Joe," Mary said. "Oh, how beautiful, and it smells so good! Amber? Go upstairs and bring down the tree stand."

"Are we going to decorate it tonight?" Lien asked.

"Sure! If you and Amber will start bringing down the boxes of lights and ornaments, we can start right now," Mary said.

Soon Amberley appeared with the tree stand, and Sam held the tree as Joe fastened it to the bottom of the trunk. The tree was almost perfect in shape and size. Amberley poured water into the stand to keep its needles fresh, and as the heat from the room warmed the tree, the strong scent of pine was everywhere. Mingled with this was the heavy, sweet smell of hot oil from the kitchen. Grandma Andrews was making her fried apple-cider doughnuts.

"Joe, you take off your coat and things and stay a while. Brenda, it would be nice if you would go out into the kitchen and make some coffee and hot chocolate to go with Grandma's doughnuts," Mary said.

Brenda smiled at Joe and took his wraps. "Well, Joe, would you like to keep me company in the kitchen?"

"I would like that a whole lot," he said, looking into her eyes. "Just let me throw a blanket over Gypsy's back."

* * *

Later that evening as the clock ticked eleven-thirty,

Brenda finished putting away the washed dishes that had been drying on the rack next to the sink before retiring to the living room to enjoy the freshly decorated tree. She had said good-bye to Joe an hour ago, and it seemed that a fresh understanding had budded between them. Brenda did not know how it would all play out, but she did know this—she was a lot happier *with* Joe than without him.

As Brenda walked through the soft glow of the living room to find a chair, she was surprised to hear Christmas music playing on the record player and to see that Sam was still up. He was sorting through his collection of arrowheads, something he liked to do when he was thoroughly relaxed.

"Daddy! I thought everyone went on up to bed?"

Her father smiled up at her. "I'm enjoying our tree. Christmastime only lasts a few days and then it's over. I want to soak up as much as I can."

"I know," she said. "I can't get over how beautiful it is. I never had a Christmas tree until I came to live with you. It's like living in a fairyland."

Brenda was silent for several moments and then spoke.

"Dad, did you set it up so Joe would come over tonight while I was out taking my walk?"

Sam smiled. "I guess it was pretty obvious. Joe wanted to bring us a tree, and I just suggested the time for him to bring it over. I was banking on you taking your walk at the usual time after supper. I know you have been hurting, sweetheart, and I just wanted to help. Joe is a wonderful guy, and I know he cares for you a lot. I can see that you two are in a quandary. Joe thinks he's not good enough for you, and you seem to be willing to sacrifice your happiness for a college education. If you two will let God handle this thing, you both might have your cake and eat it too."

Brenda smiled, looking down at her lap.

"Are we that transparent?" she asked.

"Only to everyone but yourselves," Sam answered.

Brenda looked at her father as she felt her throat swell with emotion. "Oh, Daddy, I have been so sad these last few months, but when I saw Joe tonight and heard his voice, my heart just fluttered—I . . . I think I love him!"

Sam stood up and smiled at the little girl who had become a young woman. "Well, I've seen that train coming down the tracks for quite some time. And I believe that Joe feels the same way. Now it's up to you two to let each other know—when the time is right, of course."

Sam kissed his daughter on the forehead, and with a wave of his hand, went off to bed. Brenda smiled as her eyes sparkled against the glow of the beautiful tree.

Dear Lord Jesus, she prayed, *thank You for Your tenderness and leading in my life. Thank You for Christmas and Joe and . . . for my dad!*

Four
As Long As You Are Happy

Amberley pulled the covers snugly over her head and wiggled her toes as the sunlight from the eastern sky began to glow in the bedroom window. It was Saturday, the morning after Joe's visit, and she had not slept well. Downstairs was the cheery warmth of the kitchen, hot breakfast, her family, and the Christmas tree, but she was reluctant to get up and enjoy it.

She didn't know why she felt so tired. She hoped that she wasn't coming down with a cold. Perhaps it wasn't a cold at all; maybe she was envious of her beautiful sister's ability to attract a boyfriend. *Don't boys find red-haired girls attractive?* she thought. *Perhaps my freckles and hair remind them of a strawberry, and who wants to marry a strawberry?* Whatever it was, she was ashamed of herself for feeling the way she did.

Brenda, in contrast, was busily dressing and humming to herself on the other side of the room. This only served to annoy Amberley as she scrunched her pillow tightly against her ears to block out the sound.

"Are we going to get up sometime today, sis, or what?" Brenda asked, tying her shoelaces.

Amberley peeked out at her sister from under her heavy quilt. "I'm up. I'm just thinking."

"About what?" Brenda asked.

"Is Joe coming over again this evening for supper?"

"I think so, silly," Brenda answered with a puzzled smile on her face. "You heard Ma invite him. Is that what's bothering you, Amber—that Joe and I are seeing each other again?"

Amberley sat up on the edge of her bed and let her bare feet dangle over the edge.

"I am sincerely happy for both of you," she said half-heartedly. "I think Joe is a great guy and that you were meant for each other. And as long as you are happy..."

"I *am* happy, sis," Brenda blurted out with dreamy emotion. "I didn't know how much I missed Joe until I saw him again last night. I had been treating him like a pair of old shoes because he was comfortable and went along with me on everything. I should have respected and cherished him for that, but instead—I pitied him and used him. When he told me that he'd released me to go on to college and a future with friends I could be proud of, it was like being hit with a bale of hay. The lonely months without him made me realize how much he meant to me. I know now that I wouldn't want to face the future without Joe."

A poisonous, sarcastic thought crossed Amberley's mind: *If I could find some nice guy and treat him like dirt, then maybe I would have a boyfriend too!* She looked up into her sister's smiling face and quickly stood up and put her arms around her.

"I am so sorry, sis! I *am* happy for you—I really mean that. Don't let my sour grapes ruin it for you. I'm not sure what's wrong with me."

Brenda patted her back. "The Lord will bring some nice guy into your life, Amber. I promise. Several years ago on the playground at Sodus School, when Joe and I got into that terrible fight, would you have believed that I would be dating him? We all change, sis. We all get a chance to fix things about ourselves—hopefully for the better. You are so pretty and a hoot to be with. Somewhere out there is some guy who is waiting for you and will appreciate how wonderful you are. I think you are worth it. Now, get dressed. Let's go downstairs to the land of the living and have some breakfast."

Five

Like Wildfire

Amberley was indeed happy for her sister. The sadness and gloom that had hung over her the last few months had lifted, and Brenda and Joe seemed to be an item again. As Amberley sat in her room at the blue wicker desk, she opened an old yellow folder containing the sum total of her literary output—poems, mostly, and a few short stories.

She pursed her lips as she leafed through the file. She had written a lot of poems because writing prose intimidated her. But poetry was difficult to get published unless you were a celebrity or already established, so she'd decided to send one of her short stories to a children's magazine. It had been several months since Amberley had sent it off with little hope that it would be considered, but she'd felt she must at least try.

She thought about the poet Emily Dickinson, who was a recluse and spent most of her life in Amherst, Massachusetts. She had been mostly unhappy in her life and loves, and sometimes her morose, analytical poetry bore that out.

Amberley wanted to be a professional writer but worried that unhappiness might also be her fate. She had never really been outside of Sodus Township. Perhaps seventy-five years from now, some of her personal things and a few old yellow manuscripts might make a fine display in the corner of the Sodus Library. She liked to quote her favorite Dickinson poem to herself, especially when she was sad:

> I'm nobody! Who are you?
> Are you nobody, too?
> Then there's a pair of us—don't tell!
> They'd banish us, you know.
> How dreary to be somebody!
> How public, like a frog
> To tell your name the livelong day
> To an admiring bog!

She sighed. If being "somebody" was dreary, then she had nothing to fear thus far. *Besides,* she thought, *there is sort of a strange security in being a nobody.*

* * *

The following Friday, Mary had decided to make a special supper to celebrate Jeb's retirement and welcome him into the house and his new room.

"I know it's close to Christmas, but who says you can't have two turkey dinners in December?" Mary said.

It was late afternoon, and the girls sat at the kitchen table helping Mary with the ingredients for the turkey stuffing. Lien crumbled a pan of cornbread and several loaves of white and wheat bread into small pieces. Amberley diced up onions and stalks of celery to be simmered in chicken broth, sage, sausage, and butter. When the celery and onion was soft and tender, it would be poured over the bread mixture, some to be stuffed into the turkey and the rest to be baked in a pan beside it.

Brenda was in her element when she was in the kitchen, and she would often give Amberley pointers on cooking, whether or not she asked for them.

"Don't be so bossy! I'm not Joe," Amberley teased.

"Girls, we still have potatoes to peel. Whatever we get done tonight, we don't have to rush around and do in the morning."

The girls grinned at each other. Their mother's familiar speech was often heard around the holidays.

Sam came through the back door and washed up at the sink. He wiped his hands on the dish towel hanging over the counter and sat down at the corner of the table out of the way.

"Sam, I'm going to ask Joe and Maudie for dinner tomorrow. We will have plenty to eat, and I think it would be nice for Maudie to get out," Mary said, trimming the crust on an apple pie. Maudie Schenkle was Joe's widowed mother.

"I think that's a fine idea, Mary," Sam remarked.

"I've tried to reach them on the phone all morning and I don't get an answer," Mary said.

"If you like, I can drive over now and ask them," Sam said, reaching for his hat.

"Oh, would you, Sam? I think it would be such a nice thing to have them over," she said as Sam picked up his coffee cup and truck keys off the counter.

* * *

The late morning sun, beautiful in a clear sky, was bright but deceptive. The weather report predicted more wind and lake-effect snow for that evening. Mary and the girls were busy in the kitchen, and all was going according to schedule. The turkey was stuffed and trussed and baking in the oven as Grandma Andrews set several warm pies on the counter to cool. The women had insisted that Jeb sit at the kitchen table in a special chair and relax. "This will always be your place from now on, Jeb," Mary said, handing him his coffee as he walked past.

"Thankee, Mary," he said, and shyly took his seat at the table.

Soon, Joe and Maudie Schenkle arrived. It was obvious that Maudie was not accustomed to social visits, and she shied away until Grandma Andrews took her in hand and led her into the living room for a chat. Joe smiled at Brenda and then spoke to Mary.

"Here, ma'am—from our woods," Joe said, holding up a gallon jug of pure maple syrup. "This is the last of what Pa cooked up before he passed on."

"Thank you, Joe. How sweet of you and your ma," Mary said, laughing at the obvious pun.

Brenda led Joe into the living room, and they sat side by side on the leather settee next to the Christmas tree. As they chatted, Lien brought them each a cup of coffee. Joe winked at Lien, and her face flushed red as she quickly hurried out of the room with a giggle.

Soon the dinner was ready, and the big farm in Hipps Hollow was at its holiday best. There was a hush as Sam gave thanks to the Lord for all of His provision and guidance during that long year. He also gave thanks for their faithful hired man, Jeb Sanders, whom the Lord had blessed them with these many years.

"Take a plate and sit where you can," Mary exclaimed to everyone with a smile. "I'll bet even the Pilgrims didn't have two turkey dinners back-to-back!"

Then erupted a great clattering of plates and utensils, followed by the low hum of conversation as everyone set forth to enjoy the good meal. Soon, when stomachs were full and interest in turkey began to wane, hot coffee and Grandma's pumpkin pie with its bottom layer of cheesecake were set out for anyone brave enough to attempt it.

When the low buzz of conversation resumed and the guests again retired to the large living room with their desserts and coffee, Amberley walked into the kitchen to help with the cleanup. As she began to wash the dinner dishes, Brenda and Lien covered the leftovers with wax paper but left them on the table for a later afternoon repast.

Amberley gazed out the kitchen window and noticed the bright sky of the morning hastily turning into a cold, cloudy afternoon with spitting snow. Soon, a pattern of lake-effect snow set in, familiar to everyone living around the Great Lakes. Vicious squalls of blinding, heavy snow alternated with periods of blue sky and bright sunshine.

Amberley stood at the sink with her apron on and warm suds up to her elbows. As she began to set the rinsed plates in the drying rack, she noticed again that she was not feeling well. She had a headache and felt tired. When the last dish was done, she asked to be excused. Mary felt her forehead for temperature.

"Do you feel all right, sweetheart?" Mary asked.

Amberley started to nod, then shook her head. "I'm okay, Ma. I've just been so tired lately. Maybe I'm getting the flu. It's this weather, you know."

"Go on up to bed, honey, and I'll be up to check on you," Mary said with some concern.

Amberley lumbered up the stairs. By the time she reached the landing, she had to lean on the banister for a moment. She had been tired and glum the last few days but had dismissed it along with her selfish feelings toward Brenda. But this was different. She was so weary that by the time she reached her room, she couldn't undress herself. She just lay across her bed, pulled the covers up over her face and shoulders, and fell into a deep sleep.

* * *

Amberley awoke the next morning feeling as fragile as a kitten. Mary and Brenda had finished undressing her and tucking her in the night before, but she didn't remember it. As she turned her head to look out the window, she cried out in pain. Her neck hurt tremendously on the left side. She tried to turn her head back, but the pain was almost unbearable.

I must have slept wrong to make my neck so stiff, she thought.

Amberley reached up to touch her neck and found that it was hot to the touch and swollen from her chin to the back of her jaw. She tried to get out of bed, but weakness and dizziness kept her from doing more than swinging her legs halfway out. She curled up again, closing her eyes against the dizziness.

She opened her mouth to call out for her mother, but nothing would come out. Panicked, she reached out and pushed a water glass off the nightstand onto the floor. The crash brought Mary and Brenda running up the stairs.

"Oh, dear Lord!" Mary burst out as soon as she saw Amberley. She shouted, "Brenda, call Dr. Cumberland immediately!"

Amberley looked pathetic. The left side of her face and neck was swollen like a chipmunk's with a cheek full of seeds. Her skin was red and felt as hot as a sunburn.

Soon, Dr. Cumberland arrived in his old green Rambler. "Brenda? Put a cool, damp cloth on your sister's forehead and neck." He motioned for Mary to follow him out of the room. His face was grim.

"Mary, I don't want to alarm you, but we must get her to the hospital right away. Amberley is a very sick girl."

"Why, Doctor, what does she have?" Mary asked in astonishment.

"I'm not sure yet, but if it's what I think it is, every minute we waste will be against her."

Dr. Cumberland quickly called for an ambulance to take Amberley to the county hospital in Berrien Center, and as the ambulance disappeared down the long driveway on the way to the hospital, Mary, Grandma Andrews, and the girls piled into the red Studebaker to follow it.

Dr. Cumberland had gone on ahead to ready the emergency room, and he ordered Amberley into isolation. Mary and the others waited in the small room down the hallway. Sam had to finish the necessary chores but would be along soon. An hour or so later, Dr. Cumberland walked soberly into the waiting room and began to pace the floor. "Let's wait for Sam to get here," he said.

Mary looked up at Dr. Cumberland. His white hair was unkempt, and the green three-piece suit he had worn for years was faded and hanging loosely on his bony frame. He was an old man now and should have retired years ago. Mary knew that when he was gone, no other doctor would come out to their house to treat them. Dr. Cumberland was a relic of the past. He was the only doctor she had ever known, and he had not only delivered Amberley but had also delivered Mary. Now the thought crossed her mind that he might be presiding over Amberley's home going to heaven.

"Amberley is a very sick girl," he stated for the second time as Sam sat down next to Mary. "More tests are pending, but I believe she has contracted a strain of bacteria that is attacking the soft tissues of her neck. If it's what I think it is—well, this germ spreads like wildfire!"

"But will she be all right, Doctor?" Sam asked.

The old physician took off his glasses and rubbed his tired eyes. "We are giving her antibiotics and keeping her comfortable. We are doing all we can for her now. As you are praying folk, perhaps you should enlist God's help in this matter."

"Sam?" Mary said. "I know it's Sunday morning, but will you please try to reach Pastor Mitchell?"

"I'll call him," he said.

Mary sat back in her chair, overwhelmed. *This is happening too fast! Too incredibly fast! I . . . I can't think!* Brenda sat close to her mother, and laying her head against her breast, could hear her heart pounding. Mary rested her chin on Brenda's head and held her tight.

Pastor Mitchell arrived right after the morning service and led them in prayer. "Sam and Mary," Pastor said, "the staff here are doing all they can. We can only continue in prayer. Let's leave this in the Lord's hands and trust Him to do what He thinks is best."

Six

The Waiting

The next afternoon was cold and clear. The bright sun, though low in the winter sky, was a blazing light against the fresh-fallen snow. Sam, Mary, and Grandma Andrews took turns waiting at the hospital for news on Amberley's ever-changing condition. They would all have liked to stay there around the clock, but life had to go on at the big farm. Even though the farm used an automatic milking system, someone still had to attend the chore. Milking was done twice per day, every day. The cows were brought to the milking room in small groups, in the same exact order and at the same times each day so as not to confuse them and make them anxious. Their teats and udders had to be sterilized before being attached to the milking equipment, which had to be constantly monitored. The milk had to be properly stored and cooled to prevent spoiling and then pumped into the waiting creamery trucks. It was a long, long day for anyone, and without Jeb's help, Sam quietly had to go about his duties and hurry to the hospital to be with his daughter when he could.

Sam insisted that Brenda and Lien go to school, although they were not happy about it. Mary and Grandma Andrews tried to have the meals ready as usual and at their normal times.

"Business as usual, even during times like these," Grandma Andrews said. "That's the ticket."

"The livestock still get hungry," Sam said, "and the work never goes away."

Mary stood at the kitchen window and looked out over the white fields of snow. It was a lovely day, all things considered. She thought about Amberley and how she would have loved this day at home. How she would have sat at the little table by the window with her composition book and pen.

As Mary's eyes scanned the bright horizon, they settled upon the family cemetery at the top of the old orchard hill. The headstones were frosted white, and a solitary red-tailed hawk was perched ominously above the patch of land on the bare branch of an apple tree. It peered down upon the lifeless, snowy landscape, looking for food, oblivious to any human feelings or sorrow. It was as if it too had lost its way.

My beautiful little girl, she thought. *How can I go on if her light goes out?*

* * *

It was late afternoon, and the shadows were long as Brenda buttoned up her coat and wrapped her scarf about her neck. She looked forward to her walk up the long driveway to get the mail so that, if only for a few moments, she might think of something other than her sister's illness.

The low sun in the western sky looked like a large orange ball as it forced itself to shine through the steadily thickening winter clouds. As she trudged through the crunching snow, the bitter wind cut at her. She was freezing by the time she reached the road. She found the mailbox stuffed with Christmas cards, small packages, and a seed catalog. Brenda unfolded a canvas bag from her coat pocket and raked the contents of the large country mailbox into it. Tightening the strings on the bag, she tossed it over her shoulder and began the long walk back.

Will there ever be another springtime if Amber goes away? she thought.

Just then, Joe's black pickup truck pulled up next to where Brenda was walking. He reached over and opened the passenger-side door for her, and Brenda got in.

"How are ya?" Joe asked with an empathetic smile, reaching down and squeezing her hand. "You're freezing! I thought maybe I'd go up to the hospital and sit with ya, if you don't mind."

Brenda said nothing but slid over next to Joe, holding his arm and laying her head against his shoulder. She was so very tired and heartbroken, and she had wrung her heart out in prayer to the point of exhaustion. Her feet felt like they were made of wood, and they began to sting and tingle in the heat of Joe's truck. Brenda bit her lip and rested her eyes.

"Sorry, Joe," Brenda said finally, opening her eyes again and looking up at him.

Joe paused, resolute. "I want ya to know, Brenda, that I am here for you, always, no matter what. You kin lean on me, now and forever."

Brenda smiled up at him through her dreamy, tired eyes. "Why, Joe—if I didn't know better, I'd say you just proposed to me."

Joe did not smile but gazed firmly out of his window across the snow-covered fields, his countenance again like the rough, noble Saxon knight she had come to know. "Well, I'm offerin', and when the time is right for ya, I'd like it to be me."

Seven

The New Resident

The next several days only brought more distressing news. The infection was still spreading, and Dr. Cumberland asked the family together so he could update them on Amberley's condition. There was a young man with him whom they had not seen before. He was tall and handsome and wore a traditional white doctor's coat with a stethoscope draped around his neck.

"Folks," Dr. Cumberland began, taking the man by the elbow, "this is Dr. Henry Wheeler. He is just beginning his residency here and will be working with me. If I am not here, you may direct any questions to him, and he will be able to get you an answer."

Dr. Cumberland paused as the expression on his face became serious. "I have a name for this disease that has struck our Amberley. It is known as *Necrotizing fasciitis*, or more commonly, the flesh-eating disease. It presents itself by attacking the deep layers of the skin and the soft tissues underneath. There is associated fever, swelling, pain and general sickness. It is a rare infection, and how she got it we don't know. The best treatment we can give her at this point is an antibiotics regimen and removing the infected tissue."

Dr. Cumberland cleared his throat. "Last night I took an ink pen and drew a line at the border of the infection on Amberley's neck. It has already spread beyond that line. Now, I've always been straight with you folks. This thing could affect her heart and kidneys, and if it does, she won't have the strength to get well. Many of the people who get this infection . . . don't recover."

"Oh, Doctor!" Mary asked pleadingly. "Isn't there something that can be done? This is the twentieth century, after all. We just put a man on the moon a few years back. Surely there is something?"

"I'm trying some specific antibiotics that I hope will be effective against this type of bacteria. I'm sorry that I can't allow you into the room with her. It's important that we limit physical contact to just medical staff. Now, why don't you folks go home and rest, and then you can come back tomorrow," Dr. Cumberland said tenderly.

***

Later that evening, after the supper dishes had been washed and put away, Sam and Mary sat in the living room together. They stared at the Christmas tree that had yielded them so much pleasure. Now, even with all of the beauty, shine, and glitter, it was as if the tree and Christmas itself had lost their ability to move them forever.

What a long, miserable night it's going to be! Mary thought. *My little girl is laying up there so sick and all alone.*

Sam instinctively put his arm around Mary and was quiet. Brenda and Lien had already gone up to bed, also exhausted from the long day and the news about their sister.

"Trouble!" Mary said thoughtfully, breaking the long silence of the room.

"What's that you say?" Sam asked.

"It's this trouble. Every time it comes, we take it to the Lord, and He brings us through it. The clouds seems to lift, and we feel the relief of new strength gathered, lessons learned, and our faith increased; we have learned to trust Him more. But sure enough," Mary said, shaking her head, "sure enough and without fail, looming off in the distance is another storm brewing. God lets us rest a while, but soon the trouble is back, and we begin the process all over again. It will not stop, ever—not until we die!" There was almost a sound of despair in Mary's voice.

"I guess it is God's mercy that we are only destined to live 'three score and ten.' Can you imagine what Methuselah had to endure in nine-hundred-and-sixty-nine years?" Sam asked, trying to match his wife's keen observation and eloquence.

Mary turned anguished eyes to her husband. "But it has to be for our good, Sam! It just has to be! How could we make it if we didn't believe that God was real and that everything that happens to us is with His knowledge and for our benefit?"

Sam was quiet a moment, and he tightened his arm around his wife. "It all comes down to grace, Mary. God is not dumping things on us to see how we react or how much we can take. He knows that already. He wants us to learn to handle trouble by His grace, not by our own strength—even if the worst should happen."

There were tears in her eyes. "But I feel so terrible inside, Sam! How do I get God's grace when I need it? And I need it now."

"I—" Sam started, and then cleared his throat. "'And He spake a parable unto them to this end, that men ought always to pray, and not to faint.' That's in Luke. It means . . . well, if we are not praying, we are fainting; there's no ground in between." Sam closed his eyes and swallowed hard, as deeply moved as his wife by the vision of their little girl and the terrible danger and misery she was in. His voice was dry and husky. "We must *ask*, and keep asking God to send the grace and not stop until it comes."

* * *

Amberley lay staring at the ceiling, trying to understand what was happening to her. She was terribly sweaty and warm. She knew she was very sick, but she felt nothing but euphoria. If she attempted to move her head, the objects in the room became fluid and the colors flowed together.

Dr. Wheeler fitted a mask over his nose and mouth, took the chart out of the rack on the door, and quietly walked into Amberley's room. He checked her pulse and examined the infection on her neck. She looked up but didn't recognize him. Amberley spoke in a whisper.

"You're new here, aren't you?"

"Yes, I am. I'm here to work with Dr. Cumberland. We're going to see if we can get you well again," he said, smiling.

"What's your name?" she asked, her voice light and tinged with delirium.

"Dr. Wheeler."

"No, no, no! I mean your real name!" she said.

"My name is Henry. You can call me Hank."

"Well, Hank! You look mighty handsome in your white coat!" Amberley said, reaching out to touch his sleeve.

"Thank you, Miss Bridges," he said cordially.

"No, no! You can call me 'berley!"

He smiled. "Don't you mean 'Amberley'?"

"That's what I said! 'Mberley"!"

"I know a young lady who needs her rest," Dr. Wheeler said, setting the clipboard down on the edge of the bed.

"Really? Who is she?" Amberley asked, with such a serious expression on her face that Hank Wheeler had to grin.

"You!" he said, pointing at her and trying to restrain a

chuckle.

"Ma says it's not polite to point, but I don't mind, Doctor Hank," she said, closing her eyes for a moment and finding herself nearly out of breath.

"No more talk. You take a nap now, and I'll be in to check on you later," he said, turning to leave the room.

Amberley reached out and clutched the doctor's hand with a strength that surprised him.

"Don't go, Doctor Hank. I'm so frightened!"

Hank Wheeler stopped and placed the back of his hand against Amberley's fevered cheek. "I won't leave until you fall asleep—I promise!" he said, pulling a chair up to the edge of her bed. He held her hand and noted how pretty she was as she drifted off to sleep and clouded dreams.

* * *

The next afternoon, Dr. Cumberland and Dr. Wheeler met with Sam and Mary again to update them on Amberley's condition.

Dr. Cumberland again assumed his serious face, which almost resembled a frown. "Folks, the infection hasn't yet shown signs that it is willing to abate. It has spread down her neck and to her right arm. The skin on her neck has ulcerated and separated into an open wound." He hesitated. "I must be blunt with you all. If this infection continues at its present rate, she may not make it another twenty-four hours. I'm so sorry!" Dr. Cumberland shook his head slightly in despair. Then he cleared his throat and continued.

"You know, folks, I can actually remember the day I brought Amberley into this world. I have watched her grow up and treated her tonsillitis, mumps, and every scrape and bruise you can imagine. I have been privileged to see her become a beautiful young woman."

He leaned against the back of a chair as if it were a pulpit. "But you know, the one consistent thing I have learned about medicine over the years is that it is so exasperatingly limited. Most doctors will not tell you this, but they are sometimes just as surprised as everyone else when a cure takes place. I just want you to know that I have never had a routine case—each one has had a human face on it. That's the reason, I suppose, that I still grab my black bag and come out to my patients' houses when they call. It's true that things look bad right now, but I have not written your daughter off. Not by any means. I know that you are good Christians, and I would appreciate your prayers for me as well as for your daughter."

"Thank you, Dr. Cumberland. We appreciate that more than you can ever know, and we *will* pray for you," Mary said, her voice trembling but sincere.

When the doctors left the room, Mary buried her face in Sam's shoulder and wept long and hard. Brenda sat with her arm around Lien. They were numb and scarcely able to comprehend what was happening. It was as if the oxygen had been sucked out of the room.

* * *

Hank Wheeler stood silently in the doorway of Amberley's room, watching her as she labored to breathe, knowing that any one of those breaths could be her last. She looked so helpless with the oxygen mask on her face and an IV tube attached to her arm. He felt in some strange way that the outcome of this particular case would affect him deeply all the remaining days of his career.

Amberley was nearly in a coma, and as he let the door close behind him, he began to pray. *Dear Lord, I was told in medical school not to get personally involved with my patients, because a doctor cannot bear the sorrow and still do his job effectively. If there is a way to do that, please show me, for I haven't yet been able to master it. This girl is kind of special. Please give us all of the tools we need to help her. I do need Your wisdom and grace.*

He quietly pulled up a chair next to her bed and took her hand, pondering in the silence.

* * *

Brenda put on her coat and asked to be excused from the waiting room. She opened the door and paused at the hush of new snowfall. She walked and walked up and down the lonely sidewalk in front of the hospital, tired and perplexed. When she returned, she was shocked to hear that Amberley's heart had stopped beating and that the doctors were barely able to bring her back. Mary's eyes were full of tears; Lien's face was buried in Grandma Andrews's coat. And to Brenda's horror, discussion was already being made of funeral arrangements and Amberley's burial on the orchard hill. It seemed that her impending death was a foregone conclusion. Brenda caught her breath and left again to be alone and to pray.

Dear Lord, You have done a lot of mighty things in my life. You allowed me to be part of the Bridges family. You protected me time and time again when I, by rights, should be dead now. You sent that little girl up there to be my sister and to tell me about Christ. I owe her everything. Now, Lord, please hear me out. You have created all things. You created us — very complex creatures indeed. You also created the bacteria that are ravaging my sister's body right now. I give Amberley to You and ask You to destroy those germs if it be Your will. I don't know how I can go on, Lord, if Amberley dies. All of the plans I have made for the future with Joe and college . . . all of this is nothing if she dies. Dear God, You must heal my little sister!

Brenda paused for a moment and then prayed again.

But I promise You this, dear Lord. Even if You choose to take Amberley home to be with You, I will remember the words of Job: "Though He slay me, yet will I trust in Him."

Brenda could say nothing more. Her heart had been drained, and she walked until she found a deserted, snow-covered bench. Brenda stood for a moment and then crumpled upon the wood to weep in the seclusion. *I wish Joe were here right now,* she thought as she pulled her collar up around her face.

* * *

The room was already bright with sunlight when Lien rolled over to look at her clock. It was nine-thirty in the morning, and she had overslept. She quickly sat up on the edge of her bed and rubbed her eyes. How could she still be in bed at this hour? Lien picked up her clock and noticed that the alarm button was not set. Had she forgotten to set it in her weariness last night?

Quickly dressing and combing her hair, she scrambled down the stairs to the warm kitchen. Sam and Mary were seated at the table, and they both turned to look at her as she entered the room.

"Sweetie, you don't have to get up yet. Why don't you go back up to bed and get some more rest?" Mary said.

"Ma, I'm not tired anymore. I'm sorry for oversleeping. I think I forgot to set my alarm."

Lien poured herself a glass of juice and made a bowl of hot oatmeal from the pan on the stove. As she took a sip from the glass, she noticed that her parents were not talking but sitting still, drinking their coffee. Lien listened for the familiar hum of the old electric wall clock, which sometimes made so much noise that she could hear the gears turning inside of it. But this morning, she could hear another sound, off in the distance. It was the sound of a tractor engine working hard.

Lien stood up and walked to the window. Trying to locate the sound, her eyes scanned the bright, white, sunny horizon, which was covered with a heavy frost. There across the field, high up on the orchard hill, was a blue tractor with a backhoe, busily digging a hole in the old cemetery.

Lien turned to look at her parents for an explanation when Sam stood up and put his arms around her. "We turned off your alarm, honey, hoping he would be through before you got up."

"But Dad," Lien exclaimed. "Amber's not . . . is she?"

"No, sweetie," he said. "Nothing like that, but we had to be practical. Jim is the sexton who digs all of the graves in Sodus Township, and due to the weather and the holidays, he wouldn't be able to come out for a week. We had to put our feelings aside and prepare for what might be."

Lien did not cry, but closed her eyes and let Sam hold her close. She said no more but took her juice and walked into the living room.

Mary quickly stood up to follow her daughter when Sam spoke.

Michael Leonard Jewell

"Let her go, Mary. She's a big girl now and must work through this in her own way. There will be time enough for hugs and tears later on."

Eight
The Treasures of Our Lives

The warm showers of late April had inundated the forests and wooded lots of southwest Michigan with small armies of dedicated mushroomers. These guardians of the prized fungus, who selfishly kept their most profitable locations secret from generation to generation, were having a bountiful harvest. This had been an unusual year for the spores to bloom, and many residents of Sodus Township looked forward to feasting upon the succulent morel with their roast beef and gravy.

The Bridges family were no different, and right after breakfast that morning, Sam took Lien to the hollow for her first mushroom hunt. "Lien, if you're going to be a dedicated 'shroomer, you must always put the mushrooms you find in a mesh onion sack so the spores will shake out and reseed the ground for next year," he told her. "And try to pinch them off just above the ground level so we leave some of the roots behind."

By midmorning, they had returned from the woods

with two large sacks full. Several of the spongy mushrooms were as large as a man's fist, and the thought of them sautéed in butter made their mouths water. Sam and Lien had visited the place in the woods where the memorial garden for her parents was to be made. The events of the last few months—Amberley's illness and the heavy workload of the farm—had made them tardy in beginning the project. Sam apologized to Lien and assured her that they would begin one day soon.

After the morning mushroom hunt, Sam showered and put on his good clothes to drive into Berrien Center. Mary waved at him as he drove down the long driveway, and then she sat down on the porch swing next to Grandma Andrews.

"Ah, daughter, it's as if the old place has come back to life again! There are young'uns running around, crops sprouting in the fields, strong men working hard, and young men courtin' their lady loves. I wish your pa could be here to see all of this again!" Grandma Andrews said wistfully.

Mary smiled. "I know, Mom. This is my lifelong dream finally realized."

Lien had gone to the hothouse next to the toolshed to fetch some plants, and when her wooden carrier was full, she sought out her mother, who was headed to the kitchen to help Grandma Andrews start lunch.

"Ma, will you first walk with me to the graveyard on

the hill? I want to plant some flowers there," she said, taking Mary by the hand.

"Sure, honey, but let me help you with that carrier. It looks mighty heavy."

Together they walked up the path to the family cemetery on the orchard hill. The warm April breezes were blowing softly, and the smells of clean plowed earth and fresh air filled their nostrils. Fluffy white cumulus clouds scudded by without the least intention of developing into foul weather.

Once at the top of the hill, their moods became more subdued as Lien quickly began planting flowers in front of each of the graves. She stopped to read the Vietnamese names on her parents' headstone.

Mary walked over to a recently filled-in grave next to her father's and stared at it. The yellowish-brown earth was just beginning to flush with tiny blades of newly seeded grass that looked like a bright green carpet of fur. Mary's eyes began to moisten as she moved to blot her tears with her handkerchief. *Here in this place is buried all of the treasures of our lives,* she thought, and then turned to walk back to the house with Lien.

As they descended the hill together, Sam's pickup truck drove up the long dirt-and-gravel drive, leaving a slight trailing plume of dust. Lien shrieked with joy and ran down the hill, dropping the gray wooden carrier in her wake. "They're here!" she shouted.

Sam stopped his truck in front of the door and got out.

"Well, how are we doing?" Ma asked, puffing from trying to keep up with Lien.

"Just fine! I think it will be smooth sailing from here on out!" Sam said happily.

Lien opened the passenger door, and there, thin and pale, was Amberley. Lien carefully helped her to her feet.

"Better let me help you, sweetie," Sam said. "Your muscles aren't strong enough yet."

"Daddy, I was thinking that Lien is strong enough to help me—don't you think so?"

Lien smiled at being given this great responsibility and proceeded to walk Amberley to the house.

"Sis, let me sit down on the porch. I'm not ready to go inside yet. I want to enjoy this weather. Where is Brenda, Ma?"

"Where else? She's at Joe's, helping his mother can the first pickings of asparagus. She should be along soon."

Dinnertime was a happy time as the family brought Amberley up-to-date on the doings of the farm. Several new calves had been born, and Sam was raising hogs and cattle for the freezer, taking orders from the people in town. Amberley savored every bite of food. She could not remember when she had tasted anything as good as Ma's wilted lettuce with smoky bits of bacon, fried winter parsnips pulled from the garden that very morning, golden-brown crispy bluegills from Pipestone Lake, and of course, buttery mushrooms from the beloved hollow.

When the table was cleared, Lien helped Amberley to her place on the porch where she could again look out across the open fields of the big farm. She spread out a warm blanket across her sister's lap and then, putting her finger against her chin, Lien disappeared into the house. Seconds later she returned and handed Amberley a letter.

"I almost forgot," she said. "This came for you yesterday."

Amberley read the name on the envelope.

"It's from Hank—I mean, Dr. Wheeler!" she exclaimed with a smile, and she quickly tore off the end.

Amberley had not seen or heard from the young doctor since he had taken an emergency leave to return to his home in Chicago a week ago. As she quickly scanned the two-page letter, the smile on her face faded away. Hank, or rather Dr. Wheeler, had written to tell her that he would be gone for a while and might look in on her when he returned. He had heard that she was getting out of the hospital, wished her well, and said he would write her again soon. The tone was professional and distant.

Amberley slowly refolded the letter and carefully put it back into its envelope.

"I was just his patient, then!" she said under her breath. "How easy it is to say things during moments of loneliness, knowing full well that you never really meant them."

Lien took Amberley by the hand. "What, sis?"

"Nothing, sweetie," she said, forcing herself to smile. "Would you please get me a cup of tea?"

As the screen door slammed shut behind Lien, Amberley struggled to stay in control of herself. *I guess this letter only confirms what I was afraid of. Hank's interest in me was only a professional one. All those long hours of conversation over the last few months were just two lonely people passing the time.*

Amberley held out her skinny hands and touched her face. How thin and pale she had become during the months of her convalescence! And she had an ugly scar on the side of her neck from the terrible infection. Nor was the damage only on the surface—there was a chance the illness had damaged the valves in her heart. Only time would tell. What man would be interested in a girl who was already sick and might not live out her normal life? And Hank, being a doctor, knew the chances of that better than anyone.

With resolve, Amberley lifted her head and thought, *I must concentrate on getting well. Then there is lost time to be made up at summer school, and then perhaps I will be well enough to start college in the fall.*

She could hear Lien returning with the tea and quickly sat up and wiped her eyes. Sensing that something was wrong, and after some moments of silence, Lien spoke.

"Amber, isn't Dr. Wheeler going to be your beau?"

Amberley looked at her little sister and smiled, surprised at her innocent attempt at sophistication.

"No, sweetie. I was only his patient, and that is all."

The Big Farm in Old Sodus

* * *

It was a wild, stormy evening in the northern suburbs of Chicago. The bitter northeastern winds, the backside of an early springtime gale, swirled over the Great Lakes in hurricanelike fashion. Fierce waves from Lake Michigan slammed explosively against its western shore. Gray and white gulls, driven inland by the wind and rain, were put to shame by the braver terns that fearlessly hovered above the mountains and hills of violent water.

Nestled in a well manicured wooded park near the far north side of the city sat a magnificent estate that had been occupied for several generations by the same family of prominent businessmen and lawyers. The red-brick mansion was blazing with light, and its wealthy residents, having just dined, retired to a cozy drawing room. After the servants were dismissed, the father and mother settled down to speak with their son.

"Henry, you just picked at your meal. Are you feeling well?" said the elegant lady seated in a comfortable chair. Short and petite, she was dressed in a stylish fashion with all the mannerisms of one comfortable and confident among society's wealthy and elite.

"I feel fine, Mother. I'm just not very hungry tonight," Hank answered, taking a sip of hot tea. "My mind is on my work, I guess."

His father, an older man with graying temples, crossed his legs and picked up his cup and saucer.

"Son, we don't hear much from you these days. You haven't been home in quite some time. It's unfortunate that it takes a family illness and death to bring you back. Is your residency keeping you that busy?"

"Yes, Father," Hank replied with a furrowed brow. "It is part of the price you pay to become a doctor. The man I'm assigned to is an old country sawbones, but I am continually impressed by his dedication to his patients. I wish I was more like him."

"I offered to get you a top spot here in Chicago or even New York," Mr. Wheeler said, taking a sip of tea. "Why you chose to finish up in a small-town hospital I'll never know. None of my friends at the club understand—I sure don't!"

"We've discussed this to death, Dad," Henry said. "If I'm going to be the kind of doctor I want to be, I'm not going to find the right opportunity here. I want to help people who can't afford a membership at the club."

Mr. Wheeler set his cup down, and leaning forward, peered into his son's face.

"Henry, I know how you are. You have a propensity for getting too wrapped up in the personal side of your work. Take it from someone who knows the world. You can't do that and be successful—as a lawyer *or* a doctor."

"I don't try to be, Father," Henry said, trying to understand where his father's conversation was leading. "A new doctor's time as a resident means long hours and not much sleep. Spending a lot of time with your patients just comes with the territory. You are naturally going to care for them more than usual."

Mr. Wheeler stood up and walked to the window, pausing for several moments in silence. "Let me get you a position here in Chicago, Henry. I have friends who could help you, and you would be able to live here at home."

"Thanks, Dad, but I'm happy where I am."

Craig Wheeler turned to look at his son. "Henry, I just don't want to see you get too comfortable. Who knows what crazy notions you might get caught up in? I have great plans for you. I have invited one of my partners over for supper tomorrow night. He's bringing his daughter, who is just finishing her first year in college. I want you to meet her. I hear that she is quite lovely—and eligible."

Henry tried to hide his irritation. "Dad, I don't have time to get involved with anyone right now. Besides, I would rather choose my own way and my own friends."

Craig Wheeler paused and then turned to face his son as if he was about to cross-examine a witness. "I was hoping to do this the easy way, son, but now I must be blunt. Could it be that you have more than a professional interest in one of your patients—a young woman, perhaps?"

"Craig! Please be kind," Marjorie Wheeler said softly, raising her hand in her husband's direction.

Henry turned to look up at his father as the father

looked at his son.

"What's this about, Father? Please come to the point."

Craig Wheeler hardened his jaw and then carefully chose his words.

"I'm talking about this girl from some hick town called Sodus," he said, glancing at a folded document that he had just pulled from his pocket. "I want to know what your interest is in this . . . this dirt-poor, unsophisticated hillbilly girl from Michigan. Could you seriously be interested in this person?"

Henry barely kept his seat—but he didn't bother to hide his disgust. "So you've hired a snooper to follow me. Typical of the way the Wheelers do business."

His father ignored the jab. "And isn't this so-called 'young woman' more like a young girl? You are far too old for her!"

"This girl, as you call her, is eighteen and a woman. She will be starting college this fall. There is nothing between us but friendship. And must I remind you, Father, that you are eight years older than Mother and that she was just seventeen when you first met?"

Craig Wheeler was surprised at his son's quick retort, but as a seasoned lawyer, he didn't show it.

"It was different with your mother. She was very mature and accomplished, and she came from one of the finest families in Chicago."

Henry shook his head. "So that's it! It's acceptable to rob

the cradle as long as the babe in arms is wealthy and accomplished! This 'unsophisticated hillbilly girl' is not unlike mother in a lot of ways. And not everyone from Michigan is a hick or a hillbilly. Furthermore, she *was* my patient! Now we're just friends."

Craig Wheeler, the master attorney, sought to read his son's face and body language for a few moments as he began to lecture. "Well, sir, I have it on good authority that she regards you as more than just her doctor and her friend. Much more!"

Henry stood to face his father. "Let me say it again: this woman was my patient, and we became good friends, but as to her having any further regard for me—I certainly am not aware of it."

The skepticism in his father's face was clear. "Then let me remind you, Henry, I control the money in this family, and I have the say-so about your inheritance. I will not see all of what I and your grandfathers have built be thrown away on this . . . this person. And don't forget, before you talk to me this way—I am still your father! Now mind, and that's all I have to say!"

Mr. Wheeler left the room in a huff, leaving Henry on his feet, breathing hard with agitation.

Marjorie Wheeler stood up and went to her son, putting her hand on his arm.

"Henry, dear?" she said softly. "I didn't know that he had hired a private investigator until yesterday."

"What is Father trying to do?" Henry exclaimed, turning on his mother. "Run me off like he did Richard? I will not be intimidated by him and told who I can have as a friend! I will leave him to himself and never darken these doors again!"

The mother winced. "I don't want to run your life, son. All I ask is that you be careful. If you have any feelings for this girl Amberley, that is your business. Just take it slowly. That is what your father and I did, and we have had a happy marriage."

Henry was surprised to hear Amberley's name. He narrowed his eyes. "And how did you know her name?

"Don't be too upset with me, son," Marjorie Wheeler said with a sympathetic smile. "I peeked at the detective's report too."

Nine
Keeping It Going

Since Jeb's retirement, Sam found himself getting up earlier and earlier and working late into the evening just to get the basic chores done. Milking the cows and collecting, washing, and putting the eggs into cartons was enough to keep one man busy all by himself, let alone doing the other work.

Sam first tried hiring men on a temporary basis, working them a few days at a time to keep the farm going while hoping that one of them would rise to the top like cream. But he was mistrustful of anyone who stepped foot on his farm and felt he had to watch over them constantly.

Joe Schenkle helped as much as he could, but he had his hands full working his own farm. Mary and the girls did what they could, but Sam was not about to build and maintain the farm on the backs of his wife and daughters. That was not what he wanted for them.

Jeb felt guilty about standing by and watching Sam work himself to death. One morning at the breakfast table, he spoke up.

"Sam, I feels a whole lot better now that I has these pills and am rested up. Let me hep ya some."

Sam looked at his old hired hand, who seemed to have grown even older in the months since being put out to pasture. *Good old reliable Jeb,* he thought with a smile.

"Jeb, you are retired. It's that time of life for you, and I want you to rest and enjoy yourself. Besides," Sam said adamantly in an effort to get Jeb to settle down, "no one is irreplaceable, and that includes you." But Sam didn't know if he truly believed that. He missed Jeb's dependability more and more each day.

Finally, after weeks and months of struggling and trying to hold everything together, he realized that he simply had to trust *someone,* even if they stole him blind.

Sam again picked through the names of men who had applied to fill the position, and though he mulled over the best of them, he could not hide his disappointment. Most of the men he knew by reputation: they were willing to work just long enough to get a few dollars in their pockets for some alcohol and then go skulking off in the middle of the night.

His choice was made even more difficult by the fact that Sam was not so far removed from his own history, and he understood the plight of being unable to find work because of the past. He wanted to help them all, but as a businessman, he knew he could only go so far or risk ruin for himself and his family.

The last straw came one warm afternoon when a particular hired man only worked long enough to earn the price of a bottle of wine. Sam tried to talk to him and encourage him to stick it out, but his words fell on deaf ears. Finally, in disgust, Sam paid him off—but the man demanded more, picking up a grape post that was leaning against the barn as a threat.

"I wouldn't do that, my friend," Sam said with a cool edge to his voice that let the man know he was serious. "I understand the alcohol thing—I really do—but if you think you can solve it this way, I promise you it won't work."

The man cocked his head to the side, peering at Sam through bloodshot eyes. "I wants more money. What you giv'd me is not enough."

"Sorry, pal," Sam said. "Now you had better leave."

The man paused for a few seconds, and then, holding the wooden post like a baseball bat, he swung it hard at Sam's head. Sam quickly stepped to the side, grabbing the post as it came around and using it to slam the man into the ground. Swiftly putting his knee on the man's chest and flinging the weapon off to one side, Sam gazed into the surprised face that gaped up at him.

"Now listen, buster," Sam said through his teeth, "you have two choices. Get up and leave my farm now, or go to jail—and I can guarantee you, they have no wine there!"

When Sam let the dazed man up, he said nothing but

staggered down the long driveway that led to the road. As Sam watched him disappear out of sight, he brushed off his pants and smiled. "I am getting too old for this kind of stuff," he said and walked back to the house. He didn't mention the incident to anyone.

＊＊

Later that evening after Jeb had gone to bed, Sam asked the family to gather in the living room for a meeting. When everyone was seated, Sam presided from his big chair in the corner.

"I would like everyone to listen to me for a moment. I need your help." Sam sat back in his chair, gripping the armrests on each side. "I didn't want Jeb to hear what I am about to say because he would only take it to heart and blame himself. God has been very good to us and blessed this farm, insomuch that it's going to take several men to keep it going. There are just not enough hours in the day for me to do it all efficiently and allow the farm to prosper."

"Oh, Dad," Brenda spoke out, "we can all help. Please let us!"

"Yes, Daddy!" Lien said. "I am strong enough."

"I will do what I can, Dad," Amberley said. "You can't go on like this."

Mary smiled. "What fine kids we have, Sam."

Sam reached out and took Mary's hand. "You are right

about that. I know you all want to help and have been helping the best you can, but this farm needs someone who can concentrate on the work and take ownership in it. I need someone whose thinking matches my own. What I need is another Jeb."

"Sam, if you want, I can start making inquiries around the county. Perhaps one of the old farmers knows of someone reliable," Grandma Andrews put in.

"No, Mom, but thank you. I've already done that and then some. Anybody that's any good already has a position, and what farmer is going to take a chance on having his best men pirated by another farmer? No, I have another idea."

Everyone sat quietly, waiting for Sam to speak. "Here is what I want you all to do. I want everyone here to spend a minimum of one hour each day in prayer, specifically asking the Lord to send us someone, the right someone, to be our new hand. You don't have to pray for a solid hour at a time, but throughout the day, whenever you think about it, bring the matter up to God. I believe if you will, He will hear us and help us."

As the room reverberated with the voices of his family promising to ask God for help, Sam thought back to several years before, when he'd had no way out of his problems. The Lord had certainly brought him through a lot and had blessed him with a wonderful family. He smiled. It was time to watch the Lord work again.

Ten

Karl

It had rained for three solid days when finally the weather broke, allowing the sun to shine through an all-blue sky. It had been several weeks since Amberley came home from the hospital, and she was already weary from lying around the house, reading books and thinking about Hank.

It was late morning, and she thought she might go for a walk up the driveway to get the mail—but by the time she had stepped off the porch and taken a few steps, she was exhausted. Amberley leaned against the railing near the bottom step, breathing heavily.

"Amber!" Mary exclaimed in shock. "Where do you think you are going? Do you want to end up back in Berrien General?" Mary hurried down the steps to help Amberley back to the porch swing. "Now you sit here and cover up with this warm blanket while I bring you some hot tea. The very idea!"

Amberley cooperated, but her face betrayed her frustration. "Oh, Ma. I'm so tired of being lazy and useless around the house. I wish I had someone to talk to."

"Well, I like that," Mary said. "You and I used to talk quite a bit."

Amberley smiled. "Ma, you know what I mean. You don't have time to sit around and keep me company any more than the rest of the family. Even Grandma Andrews is too busy. Will she ever slow down?"

"Probably not, but we will all 'slow down,' as you say, soon enough. Then you will look back on these days. Don't live your life in such a way that you hurry to get each day over with. You haven't worked on your writing in a long time. How about I bring you your things?"

"Sure, Ma. That would be nice. Perhaps a fit of inspiration will come over me," she teased.

"Now don't be saucy. I've read some of your stuff, and you're good. You should write some every day whether you feel like it or not," Mary said firmly.

"I know. Once I get started it seems to flow, but the trick is getting started. I wonder how Emily handled that problem?"

"Who?" Mary asked, turning to go back into the house.

"Just an old friend, Ma."

Amberley wrapped the blanket around herself and shivered. She had worked up a sweat trying to escape from the monotony of her convalescence, and now she was cold. It was one of those typical spring days on the eastern shore of Lake Michigan. The sky was deep blue, the sun was bright, and the few clouds, like puffs of cotton, raced swiftly and low across the sky. But looks were deceptive. What should have been a warm, pleasant day was chilly and uncomfortable as the wind blew across the deep, cold lake waters. Mary brought out a pot of hot tea and a few oatmeal cookies with Amberley's composition book and favorite pen. The tea was good, and after a few sips, she felt better.

Again, her thoughts drifted to Hank. She tried to make excuses for him and for herself, but the fact that he had not contacted her except for a stodgily written get-well card only frustrated and upset her. *And what do I have to offer him?* she thought. *Wouldn't he be more interested in someone nearer his own age—educated and professional? I'm sure there are plenty of beautiful lady nurses and doctors around. Hank could have his pick.*

Taking another sip, Amberley carefully picked up her composition book and opened it to where she had left off before her illness. Reading the last few lines she had written, she couldn't help thinking to herself—*What drivel!*

Then she thought, *Not everyone is going to want to read what I write. But perhaps a few will. This will be for them.* Amberley took her pen and began to write, and soon she had drifted away into the special little world she had created just for herself.

The Big Farm in Old Sodus

* * *

Sam had gone to the hardware store in Eau Claire for a bag of nails, and while he waited at the wooden counter for the clerk to ring up his order, a man approached him from behind.

"Good morning, sir! Aren't you Mr. Bridges?"

Sam turned to see who had addressed him. There stood a tall, handsome young man with short brown hair and a clean-shaven face. He carried a green army duffel bag slung over his shoulder, and his speech betrayed the fact that he had spent some time in the military. His smile was captivating and looked as if it belonged permanently on his face.

"My name is Karl. Karl McNee," he said, greeting Sam with a crisp handshake. "I heard about town that you were looking for help."

Sam looked the young man up and down, trying to get an impression of who he was. "That's right. I'm in need of a farmhand."

"I was raised on a big farm in Wisconsin before I went off to the war. I spent a couple of years in 'Nam, but that was a while ago. I thought about making a career out of the army, but it wasn't what I wanted. I just got my discharge from Fort Campbell and was visiting some friends in the area. I was with the rangers there. I hear you were in the Special Forces," Karl said, still smiling.

"That's right," Sam answered blandly after a long

pause, still trying to size the young man up. "If you are interested in applying for the job, let's go over to the coffee shop and have a chat."

Sam waved good-bye to the clerk, and putting the bag of nails behind the seat of his truck, he sat down with Karl at a back table in the tiny restaurant. "Coffee?" he asked Karl, and ordered one for himself. Sam noted a particular look on Karl's face as the smell of food drifted out from the kitchen.

"If you don't mind me asking, when was the last time you had something to eat?" Sam inquired.

"Uh, I'm fine, sir. Don't worry about me."

Sam smiled slightly. "You can level with me, Mr. McNee. I hear your stomach growling from over here. I'm thinking about having a cheeseburger and some fries. I dislike eating alone. Would you join me? I'm buying."

Karl smiled and shrugged his shoulders. "I am a little hungry, sir."

Sam ordered the food and watched as Karl wolfed it down as if he hadn't eaten in a week. Two pieces of pie and a tall milkshake later, Karl sat back in his chair.

"Thank you, Mr. Bridges. I hate being a moocher, but the truth is, I haven't had any decent chow since I left Kentucky."

"I can see that," Sam said. "Didn't they give you some cash when you got out?"

"Yes sir, but it didn't last long. I had bills to pay, you

know. That's why I need a job. I was hoping that maybe you could help me out with that."

Sam took another sip of coffee and looked intently at Karl. "The job pays $75 a week to start, and I provide room and board. The day begins at 0500 hours with the milking and then breakfast with my family. After that, there are eggs to gather, wash, and pack; stalls to clean; cows to feed; things to repair and maintain; ground to plow; seeds to plant and cultivate; and hopefully soon, crops to harvest. Add to that list about a thousand more things that I can't think of right now and one or two emergencies that will probably develop each week. We work until noon on Saturday, with Sundays off except for the milking, feeding, and egg gathering, which never end. There are several holidays that we celebrate around here, and if you last that long, I'll tell you what they are. If you work for me, you will be treated like family, and I expect you to conduct yourself accordingly."

"That sounds fair, Mr. Bridges," Karl said. "I think it's what I've been looking for."

"But first, I need to make a few inquiries before I can officially hire you. Is that going to be a problem?"

Karl shook his head. "No, sir. I understand."

"If I do hire you, you can drop the 'sir' and just call me Sam," Sam said, reaching across the table to shake Karl's hand. Then, still gripping Karl's hand firmly and with the smile fading from his face like the sun going behind a dark cloud, Sam spoke soberly. "I have three daughters I am particularly fond of. I will expect you to treat them at all times as ladies and consider your language and conduct around them. Is that understood?"

"Yes . . . yes, sir!" Karl said, squeezing Sam's hand firmly.

"Then you can have your hand back," Sam said with a smile and a nod. "In the meantime, I will show you around the farm. You are welcome to come spend the night and have supper with us."

* * *

The next morning, Sam contacted a few old friends at Fort Campbell about Karl McNee. Karl had been a staff sergeant and spent several tours in Vietnam, was ranger qualified, and had been given an honorable discharge, but that was all that anyone could really tell him. Karl was known to be particularly friendly but also seemed to keep to himself a lot.

There is no law against that, Sam thought, hanging up the phone.

Sam grabbed his hat off the peg and went to speak with Karl. Sam had put him up for the night in Jeb's old cottage, and he was waiting there to hear from him. Karl had eaten supper the night before and breakfast that morning with the family. When Sam introduced him to everyone, Karl seemed momentarily disturbed when he saw Lien come to the table. He was cordial to her, but as he ate, he watched her out of the corner of his eye. Sam noticed this and decided to confront him about it before hiring him officially.

Sam knocked on the door to the cabin and then walked in. Karl was seated on the edge of the bed, his arms folded. He was deep in thought, and when he saw Sam, he turned on his big smile as if with a light switch.

"Karl?" Sam said, removing his hat and finding a chair. "Let's talk."

"Yes, sir," he said, unfolding his arms and facing Sam.

"I spoke with some old friends at Campbell, and you were given an a-okay."

Sam looked at Karl's face and noted his obvious sense of relief, almost as if he was surprised to hear it. "But before we go any further, I would like to discuss a few things. I know you spent several years in 'Nam and that was a while ago. Is there anything particular you would like to tell me about it?"

Karl looked surprised at first and then screwed his eyes up into a tight gaze, as if he was rapidly perusing in his head the several years he had spent there.

"No, sir," he finally said. "I suppose I didn't have it any worse or better than anyone else. Why do you ask?"

"I noticed last night, and then at breakfast this morning, that you seem to be a little troubled by the presence of my daughter Lien. Is the fact that she is Vietnamese going to be a problem? I want you to be honest with me if it is."

"No, Mr. Bridges. I was surprised to see her, I will admit, but she is your business, not mine. I am just looking for a place to hang my hat and settle down."

Sam was silent for a few moments, looking at Karl. There was something about this whole thing that bothered him, but then, he was naturally suspicious. He wanted to be fair to Karl, but his family came first. "Okay, Karl," he finally said, "I'll let you show me what you've got. Mrs. Bridges has some paperwork for you to fill out. When you are through, come out to the barn and I'll get you started." Sam stood up and offered his hand. As he watched Karl walk to the house, Sam rubbed his jaw and gave his head a quick shake.

I hope I have this figured right, he thought, *and I'm not just hiring him because I'm desperate for help.*

* * *

After two weeks had passed, Karl had quickly come up to speed. He had established an efficient routine for himself and was able to do the morning and evening milking and chores faster than Sam and Jeb could do together. The stalls were cleaned and the stock fed and watered. Sam was impressed but still wary. After mulling over his thoughts for a few days, he thought he would ask Mary her opinion.

"What do you think of him, Mary?" Sam asked, stopping by the kitchen in the middle of the afternoon for a short break.

Mary took off her rubber gloves and vented the steam on her pressure cooker. She had just finished canning her last batch of asparagus. "I think he is wonderful! He's so nice and polite, and Amber and Brenda are just crazy about him," she answered. "After lunch today, he brought Amber a bunch of wildflowers from the woods while she was on the porch swing to cheer her up. I think she was happy to have someone show her some attention."

"Well, maybe," Sam said. "He is a charmer, I'll give you that, but I just hope he's not too good to be true."

Mary looked surprised. "Why, Sam! Karl seems to be the perfect guy you've been looking for to replace Jeb. Perhaps he is the answer to our prayers. Why are you so suspicious?"

Sam shook his head. "I can't say I'm sure. I know that sometimes when a man is hired, he gives you his best for the first thirty days and then starts to unravel after that. After ninety days, you start to see what the real man is like. I guess I'm just waiting for the other foot to fall." Sam stood and put his cup in the sink. "You know how I am, Mary. But I'll let Karl stand on his own merit. And you're right: he does, on the surface, seem to be what we have been looking for."

Eleven
Lien Confides in an Old Friend

The last few days of school were fast approaching, and with them the excitement and contemplation of a long summer reprieve from books and classes. The month of May had always been a tonic to those stricken with cabin fever, and this spring was no different. The hollow was again invaded by trekkers seeking to trade the cold and frost of a long, hard winter for the scent of wildflowers and greening moss.

Lien knew that in a few days, Sodus School would be dismissed, and she would rarely see her friends until the fall—if at all. At morning recess, she sat on the swings with her old friend Billy Gussette. They were about the same age. She had met him for the first time shortly after she arrived in Sodus. She had thought he was a strange little boy then, one who seemed to be the perpetual victim of every bully who ever attended school. He was always brave and tried to fight back, but he was not big enough to defend himself. She'd always felt a special kinship with him, though, because his father, a deputy sheriff, had been killed while trying to stop a bank robbery in Benton Harbor many years ago. Although Billy was still small for his age, Lien no longer thought him strange. The years of being picked on had made him tough and fearless. But he was also honest and kind.

"Billy, what are you going to do this summer?" Lien asked.

"I don't know; maybe spend some time at my Grandpa's farm. He's got lots of horses and stuff. I always enjoy it there. What are you gonna do?"

"My dad is going to make a special garden in the hollow to honor my folks who died there. But he has been so busy on the farm lately. I hope we will be able to start on it as soon as school is out," Lien answered.

Billy twisted around in the swing and then stopped to face Lien. "That's great, Lien. I hope I'll get to see you sometime this summer, and I hope you will always be my friend. I will miss you until school starts again."

"You know I will, Billy, and I will miss you too. You have always been my pal." She smiled as she kicked the gravel beneath the swing. "Billy? Can I ask you a question?"

"Sure. What is it?"

"Billy, does it bother you that I am Vietnamese?"

Billy was surprised. "What a strange question to ask. Why, I loved you since the first time I saw you that winter when we went sledding on Chapel Hill!"

"Do you really love me, Billy?" Lien asked with a chuckle.

Billy looked affronted. "Why, I always thought you were my best girl, and I might just marry you someday, just as soon as I get that job at the sheriff's department. I hafta be able to support you, ya know."

Lien and Billy both laughed out loud, and Lien playfully punched him on the arm.

"You are truly my best friend, Billy. I would miss you terribly if you ever went away."

"Then what's this stuff about being Vietnamese?" Billy asked more seriously.

Lien pressed her lips together and frowned. "Well, there's this new man Dad hired, and I don't think he likes me. I don't think he likes anybody with eyes like mine." Billy noticed how painful it was for Lien to say those words, and he frowned.

"Why do you think he doesn't like you? Does he talk mean to you or somethin'?"

"That's the problem, Billy. He doesn't say anything to me. He is friendly with both of my sisters but just ignores me. I think he hates me."

"Did you tell your father or mother? Maybe they could help."

"I don't want to do that. I need to handle this myself," Lien said thoughtfully. "If he doesn't like me for me, that's okay. But if he hates me because I remind him of the war in Vietnam . . . well, I don't know how to handle that. He is a good worker, and my parents really like him. Dad has worked so hard since Jeb retired, and I wouldn't want to do anything to run off his hired hand."

Billy reached out and put his hand on Lien's shoulder. "Well, all I know is that I like your eyes just fine. You are that pretty, and he is wrong to treat you this way. Do you want that I should talk to him?" Billy squinted his eyes with such grown-up sincerity that Lien could not help but smile.

"No, Billy. You are a good friend, but I must deal with this myself." The bell rang, and they both stood and walked to the schoolhouse.

"And d'know what, Billy?" Lien asked with a modest smile. "If you marry me someday, I might just marry you back . . . after you get that job as a sheriff's deputy, of course."

Twelve
Setting Matters Straight

It was early June and a particularly warm and windy day. At midmorning, Amberley sat on the porch swing with Grandma Andrews, peeling apples for pies. The addition of Karl to the dinner table made it necessary that they make more food.

"He has the appetite of a hardworking man, so we must turn it up a notch," Grandma said with a chuckle. "With all these pies, I just hope we can get him out of the kitchen and back to work."

"Well, Grandma, if he doesn't go, you can always throw some more shotgun shells into the stove," Amberley said, making reference to an old tale about Grandma when she was a young woman.

"Now, Amber, are you not going to be letting me forget that?" Grandma said, attempting to hide a smile and standing up to take both bowls of peeled apples into the kitchen.

Amberley poured herself another cup of tea and sat back to continue her writing when she noticed Karl walking up to the porch with the mail in his hand.

"Good morning, Miss Amber," he said, touching the bill of his hat. "Here is the morning mail."

"Why, thank you, Karl. How nice of you."

"Miss Amber, I am almost caught up with my chores. How would you like it if I harnessed up Gray and took you for a buggy ride this afternoon? I know you must get awful anxious just having to sit all day."

Karl's invitation took Amberley completely by surprise. "I . . . I must think about it. I'm still a little under the weather, you know, but thank you for the asking," she said as Karl smiled and touched his hat again.

"Just let me know if you need anything," he said, returning to his chores.

Amberley touched her pen to her chin and watched Karl as he walked away. *I must be careful,* she thought.

"Is anything wrong, Amber?" Brenda asked, picking up the mail from Amberley's lap and sorting through it.

Her sister's sudden presence startled her and brought her back to the surface. "Why, no! What could be wrong?" she said, quickly feigning concentration upon her composition book.

"Oh, nothing. I just saw you talking to Karl," Brenda answered with a serious look. As she sat down beside Amberley, she nudged her with her arm. "Well, looky what I have here!" Brenda said, waving an envelope back and forth between her thumb and forefinger. "It's from Hank!"

Amberley snatched the envelope from Brenda and opened it. It was at least seven or eight pages long, and she quickly scanned the letter, not sure of what she was looking for. It seemed that Hank would be back in Michigan, resuming his duties at Berrien General, the following week. He said he would stop by and see her.

Amberley held the letter in both hands and then carefully folded it up. "Hank's coming here next week for a visit on his way back to the hospital," she said. "I didn't expect that."

"Is that all, sis? He could have said that much on a postcard."

"Oh, he was just catching me up on what he's been doing in Chicago. Hank's a very busy guy."

"Well," Brenda said, "Joe's coming over for lunch today, so I'd better get busy helping out in the kitchen. I'll leave you to your letter."

Amberley casually waved to Brenda and unfolded the pages again.

Just when I thought it might be over, she thought, *it all comes rushing back again!*

* * *

It was the last week of classes at River School, and graduation would be on Friday. Mary had planned an afternoon picnic in the backyard to celebrate this milestone in

Brenda's life. It would be bittersweet, of course, because Amberley could not graduate.

"Are you going to be okay, sis?" Brenda asked Amberley that Friday morning. "Perhaps it wasn't a good idea to have a picnic."

Amberley sat on the edge of her bed. "Nonsense! It's not all about me. You should be honored for your accomplishment. I'm just a little behind now, but I'll meet you this fall in college. I'm looking forward to starting summer school next week."

"It just doesn't seem fair, somehow," Brenda said thoughtfully, staring out the window of their bedroom.

"How is Joe taking it? Does he know you have decided to attend a local college?"

"I have made a point of being open with him about it. No more mind games. I told him that I wanted to attend college here so I could be near him," Brenda said.

"How did he react?" Amberley asked as she got up to lay out her clothes.

"He just grinned," Brenda answered. "I know it made him happy. I want him to be able to settle down and concentrate on his farm. I never imagined that one day I might be a farmer's wife!"

"Brenda, you could have been anything you wanted to be. I wonder if Joe has a clue what a wonderful girl he is getting?"

Brenda smiled and stood up. "You are too kind, sis, but

I know what a wonderful guy *I'm* getting, and that's all that matters now. See you downstairs."

* * *

Karl continued to amaze them all with his hard work and diligence on the farm. After months of struggling along, the place began to take on the appearance of a well-oiled machine. Karl, among his many skills and talents, was an experienced mechanic, and he completely overhauled the engine on the John Deere tractor. Everything seemed to be operating at peak efficiency on the big farm, and Sam could not have been more pleased with the work ethic of his hired man.

However, Sam noticed that Karl was still not particularly friendly toward Lien. He would walk past her without speaking a word and sometimes ignored her if she spoke. He didn't seem to do this with the other girls. He was quick to bring flowers and the mail to Amberley and wash the Studebaker for Brenda, but when Lien asked him to bring her some cracked corn for her bird feeder, he abruptly told her he didn't have the time. He wondered how much Lien had noticed.

Sam could not help but wonder if Karl was still harboring a deep resentment toward the Vietnamese people due to the war. It had been several years since Karl had been in combat, but Sam had seen it many times before. Some guys could not let it go and would simply crack up at the sight of an Asian face when they got stateside. Some were moved to violence. There were deep waters flowing there, and even though Karl was a great worker, Sam had to think of Lien. This was her home, and he wasn't about to have her live in an atmosphere filled with hostility.

***

Thursday morning the following week, Amberley was up before the sunrise. She took her bath and stumbled in the dark getting dressed, trying to avoid waking Brenda. Suddenly the light went on. Brenda was sitting up in her bed. "Is that better?" Brenda asked.

"I'm sorry, Brenda," Amberley said sheepishly. "I just couldn't sleep any longer. Hank will be here early, and Ma has asked him to stay for dinner."

Brenda hugged her knees and smiled. "I know. I would be on pins and needles myself. But you never did tell me. Is this a social visit from your doctor, or does he actually have something to say?"

"Hank's not my doctor! He is Dr. Cumberland's assistant," Amberley snapped.

"Whoa! Don't be so touchy, sis. I didn't mean anything by it."

Amberley sighed and ran a brush through her red hair. "I'm sorry, Brenda. I'm just a little irritated. Sakes, how a guy can go on for eight pages and say nothing! It must be something he learned to do in medical school."

* * *

It was almost ten o'clock, and the men were busy with their chores around the farm. Mary and Grandma Andrews and Brenda were in the kitchen peeling potatoes and preparing several fat chickens to roast. Amberley had put on her best dress, and Mary had shooed her out of the hot kitchen to rest on the porch swing. Lien wanted to sit with her, but Mary found chores for her to do. She understood that Amberley needed to be alone.

Hank should have been here by now, Amberley thought, smoothing out her dress. *If he doesn't get here soon, I am going to faint!* As Amberley sought to deal with her nervousness, she saw a cloud of dust coming up the long driveway. It was a dark blue BMW sedan that she did not recognize. It parked near the end of the porch, and a tall man wearing blue jeans, a polo shirt, and a tan barracuda jacket got out. It was Hank. Amberley was so accustomed to seeing him in a suit or his white doctor's coat that she was surprised at how much he looked like a simple guy from the country. She liked the change.

Amberley stood up, putting her hands behind her and then folding them in front. Hank stepped up onto the porch, beaming a smile.

How handsome he looks! she could not help thinking.

Hank paused for a moment, and then, leaning forward, he took Amberley's hand.

"It's been a while," he said, giving her a small package wrapped with plain brown paper and string. "I thought you might like this. It's a very old volume of poems by Emily Dickinson, and I think it's an original edition. At least, that's what the bookmonger told me."

Amberley thought back to the long conversations they'd had together while she was in the hospital, discussing everything from classical literature to the Bible. He had evidently remembered her love of Dickinson. *At least he hears me,* she thought.

"Thank you, Hank. I will enjoy it. Please sit down," she said, setting the gift on the table before her. Amberley had rehearsed a little speech that she was going to give to Hank when she first saw him in an attempt to determine just what their relationship was—but for the life of her, she couldn't remember it.

"How have you been feeling?" Hank asked, leaning forward to look at her neck. "Some scar tissue, but it appears to be completely healed. Anything else?"

Amber backed away a little, covering her neck shyly. "Just a little weak still, but I'm getting stronger every day."

"I think you will be fine," he said, smiling, and then he paused. "That's a nice dress, Amber. You are quite fetching."

Amberley smiled and looked away with a blush but said nothing. Hank was charming her, and it was working.

"And something sure smells good from the kitchen. Roast chicken?"

"Yes," she answered. "I noticed you liked chicken when I was in the hospital. Remember when you would bring your plate into my room and we would eat together? I miss that." Suddenly filling with emotion, Amberley hung her head so that Hank couldn't see her tears.

Hank's face changed to that of a concerned doctor. Reaching forward, he checked her pulse and held his hand against her forehead. "You are a little warm. You haven't been trying to walk around or do too much, have you?" he asked.

"Certainly not!" she answered abruptly. "There is nothing wrong with me, Hank, and I don't need a doctor right now!"

Hank sat back in his seat and paused.

Amberley wiped away a stray tear and looked into his eyes. "Hank, I feel like I've been receiving mixed messages from you. All of those long talks we had in the hospital, the things you said to me. Was it just my imagination?"

Hank turned his head and looked off into the distance and into Amberley's deep blue eyes. "I told you once that I would always be honest with you, Amber. Do you really want to hear it?"

Amberley said nothing, but her silence showed her answer.

"I've been getting a lot of static from my parents. Not my mother, really, but my father. He's a hard-as-nails Chicago attorney, and he got wind of us—he was checking up on me without my knowledge. He knows of our friendship and how young you are. He's also quite prejudiced against anyone from rural Michigan. I have tried to talk to him, but he will not listen. Father has the idea that you consider me more than just a friend."

Amberley was stunned and embarrassed to hear the secret thoughts of her heart so rapidly unveiled. She *had* thought of Hank as more than just a friend.

"And to be totally honest, Amber, Father is suspicious of you. Although he has never met you, he thinks you are just after his son to see what you can get."

Amberley's eyes got big, and her mouth dropped open at Hank's words. She had never heard anyone accuse her of such a terrible thing, especially of something that had honestly never crossed her mind. She had wanted to know the truth about what was bothering Hank, and now here it was —both barrels. She was completely humiliated and taken aback by his severe honesty. Finally able to take a breath after a few moments, she looked into Hank's face and felt her eyes tear up again.

Seeing that his words had devastated her, Hank reached out to take her hand in his. "I'm so sorry, Amber. I didn't mean to hurt you. Please don't cry." Hank picked several tissues from the box on the table and wiped her eyes. "Now blow," he said, wiping her nose. "I don't know how to talk to women. Guys just tell it like it is, and that is that. I don't know how to sugarcoat things very well. Maybe it's the doctor in me."

After a few moments of composure, Amberley cleared her throat. "You need not sugarcoat anything for me, Dr. Wheeler, and perhaps I shouldn't sugarcoat anything for you. I *had* gotten the idea that we were more than just friends, but I was foolish and wrong. We come from two different worlds. I don't want to be responsible for any friction between you and your father, and he is right, I am a poor country girl—dirt-poor and unsophisticated. You could never be happy with that, and in the end, you would despise me too. I am a nobody, and I know my place and station in life. I need to stay there where it's safe and where I belong."

Amberley let her hand slowly slip from Hank's. She hadn't meant to say so much. But all the pent-up feelings that had been brewing since her illness just had to come spilling out.

Hank leaned forward gently. "Amber, what I told you about my father is how *he* feels—not how I feel. Doesn't the fact that I'm here mean anything to you? Besides," Hank said, his eyes looking into hers, "I really have missed you."

"I want you to be happy, Hank. But I could not have anything to do with a man—your father—who is so unfair and who hates me so much."

Hank reached out and took Amberley's hand. "I told my father that we were just friends because he is just so arrogant and cocksure of himself. I do care about you, but my feelings—our feelings—are none of his business!"

Amberley wiped her nose with a tissue and turned to look into Hank's eyes. "Perhaps you should just go. It would be best for everyone concerned."

"So you are sending me away, not giving me a chance to redeem myself—and without chicken dinner, I might add?"

Amberley couldn't help but smile. "You may stay for dinner. I know you have a long, hard shift ahead of you at the hospital tonight."

* * *

Late in the afternoon, just before supper, Sam had returned from several errands in town. On his way into the house, he stood beside his pickup truck and watched Karl walk across the barnyard to get the tractor.

Sam had been dwelling for quite some time on the problem of Karl and Lien. He liked Karl and thought he was one of the finest workers he'd ever known. He was honest and of fine character, but he just didn't seem to be able to get past his ghosts from the war. Sam understood—he had them too. He had handled his, at first, with the bottle, until his salvation and relationship with Christ changed all of that. But even so, vivid memories would come back of things he'd seen and done, causing him to flee to the Lord continually for grace to help.

Karl indeed had his ghosts, whatever they were. And his relationship with Lien, or rather, lack of one, was having an effect upon her. She was starting to avoid him, and she would ask to be excused from the table after picking at her food. She was spending more and more time in her room alone. Sam had hoped that Karl would eventually take a liking to Lien, but he had not. The time had come for Sam to take action for her sake.

He sighed heavily. There was nothing else he could do. Karl would have to go.

Thirteen
Lien Takes Matters into Her Own Hands

The heat and humidity of mid-June were taxing. Brenda was in the kitchen helping Mary and Grandma Andrews fix dinner, and Amberley sat quietly in her place on the porch swing. She was not the least interested in her writing, and she brooded over her disappointing attempts to attend summer school. The last time she had tried, just a few days before, she had needed Brenda to come and bring her home, dripping with perspiration and nausea. Any hopes of starting college that fall were fast dwindling away. She was not getting well as quickly as she should. A voice deep inside whispered that perhaps she would be sickly and invalid for the rest of her life.

Adding to her misery, Amberley couldn't help thinking about Hank and his recent visit. She had boldly sent him away, but secretly, she wished he hadn't gone. She figured that he wouldn't be back, but she couldn't stop herself from looking for his card or letter every day. Hank's father had accused her of being too young and immature. She had only confirmed his notions by acting just that way. The reality was that Hank had done nothing wrong—she was making him pay for what his father had said. *Yes, Hank! You run and keep on running! I don't blame you,* she thought. She wiped a tear away from her eye and gazed out over the fields, feeling deeply sorry for herself.

***

Karl busied himself in the barn, attempting to finish his chores before the heat of the day became too uncomfortable. He slipped on his rubber boots, and with pitchfork in hand, began to shovel out the soiled stalls. Stopping several times to wipe his face and drink from the army canteen he carried on his belt, Karl opened several windows to get a cross breeze in the thick, stifling air of the cow barn.

Suddenly, a large stack of hay fell out of the high loft above, striking Karl on the head. "What the—" he said, brushing the dry, dusty hay out of his hair with his fingers. Karl could hear a soft giggle from above, and he stopped to look. "Who's up there? Come down this instant!"

A grinning face peeked down at him, its details obscured by the beams of sunlight in the high loft. "You up there! Come down here right now, or I'll come up after you!"

The figure stood up and shinnied down the long wooden ladder to the barn floor. Karl was surprised to see that it was Lien.

"Now, what's the idea, kid?" Karl said, not amused and still pulling hay stems out of his hair. "Is this your idea of a joke?"

"So you're talking to me now, are you? I figured you couldn't ignore me if I dumped a pile of hay on your head," Lien said, laughing. "You look so funny!"

"And you're a little brat, did you know that?" Karl said sharply.

"And you are very rude! Did you know that?" she said, not laughing anymore. "I've tried to be your friend since you got here, and you treat me like I'm not a real person. Why don't you like me?"

Karl wiped the dust and sweat from his face. "I haven't got anything against you, kid," Karl said, pausing. "It's just . . ."

"It's just that I'm Vietnamese?" she said, finishing his sentence.

Karl looked at Lien, wiping a speck out of the corner of his eye. He was surprised at having his thoughts put into words. "No, kid, it's not that, exactly. I have nothing against you personally, but . . . but I lost a lot of friends over there."

Lien stood up straight and slid her hands into the pockets of her bib overalls. "I can understand that, Karl, but what does that have to do with me? Did you think I would hide in the rice paddies and shoot at you as you walk by? Or maybe I could wear my black pajamas and peasant hat and tote water for you while you work?"

"Oh, come on, kid. I didn't mean that. Be fair," Karl said, fidgeting a little. He found it strange to be dressed down by a young girl.

"Be fair? Maybe it's you that's not being fair! Maybe it's you that I should be afraid of! And in case you are interested, I lost a lot of friends over there too—and family."

With that, Lien turned on her heels to exit the barn, but she abruptly stopped at the door, turning again to face Karl. "And by the way—stop calling me *kid!*" she shouted with all her might, leaving Karl standing with his mouth wide open.

* * *

Several days passed as Karl made an effort to be kind to the young girl who had called him out. He smiled at her often and spoke to her at meals, and one evening, he made a rabbit hutch out of wood and galvanized wire screening, purchasing two rabbits—one black and one white—for her from a local farmer. Lien was polite and said, "Thank you, Karl," but it was obvious that her feelings had been deeply hurt. She was going to make Karl work for this one.

Sam was quietly pleased that Karl had finally warmed to Lien, but he also noted the cold shoulder that she had turned toward him. Wondering if the two would ever get it right, Sam hit upon an idea.

The next Saturday morning after breakfast, Sam asked Karl to remain behind to speak with him. "Karl, I have a project I want you to help me with. We don't have to do it all at once—just here and there in our spare time. I've been trying to start on it since early spring, but we have been so busy. There is a special place in the hollow that I want to make into a sort of a garden for the family. Later, maybe, I'll build a gazebo out there, but for now, I need to have the area cleaned up and made ready for plants and shrubs—that sort of thing."

Karl took a sip of coffee, listening intently to the strange request.

"You don't have to start on it today, but I thought I'd show you where it was. Why don't you hitch up the horse and buggy? It's a nice morning for a ride."

Karl trotted Gray out from his stall and hitched him to the black buggy, pulling him up to the porch steps in the shade to wait for Sam.

Sam, meanwhile, called for Lien, who was helping Brenda straighten up the living room. "Sweetie, I need you to do me a favor. I just remembered some errands I have in town. Would you go with Karl and show him the place in the hollow? He is going to help me with the garden that we are going to make there, but first, it needs to be cleaned up. Please go with him and show him exactly where it is." With that, Sam left the room, leaving his daughter standing there in surprise.

Lien slowly opened the screen door to the porch and let it close softly. There was Karl, seated in the buggy and holding the leather reins.

"Karl? Dad remembered some things he had to do. He wants me to show you the place in the hollow," she said softly, climbing up into the buggy. Karl said nothing but gave the reins a shake, signaling Gray to take the rough dirt path to Hipps Hollow.

"Which way from here, Lien?" Karl asked.

Lien pointed and then said, "That's the first time you called me by my name. And you pronounced it right too."

"I've known a lot of Liens. It's a popular name in 'Nam."

"Do you have to call it that?" Lien said, letting her irritation show. "It's called *Viet*nam."

Karl sat up a little straighter. "It's a common saying, and I didn't mean anything by it. Are we going to be cross for the whole trip?" Karl slowed the buggy down to avoid a few low-hanging branches.

Lien smiled at him. "No, I guess not."

As the buggy approached the place near Love Creek, Lien held up her hand to Karl. "Stop here!"

"Whoa, boy!" Karl said, pulling gently back on the reins. Karl surveyed the area around him. It was thick with vines, trees, and shrubs, but in one high spot there was a large pile of old, dead pine boughs and tree branches.

"It looks like what's left of somebody's hooch. Instead of bamboo, they've used pine boughs. What kind of an idiot would try to live out here?" Karl said sarcastically.

"I would . . . and my parents," Lien said softly. "My parents died here."

Karl sat back in his seat, the wind taken out of his sails, and looked at his passenger as she told him the whole story of the night when her parents had burned to death on that very spot, trying to save their only daughter. Lien closed her eyes tightly so as not to weep, but the little warm drops began to escape. Karl took his thumb and wiped away the several tears that traced down her cheeks.

"Well, it looks like I did it again," he said. "I stuck my foot in my mouth. It sounds like your folks loved you very much. Now I know why Sam had you come with me. He sure is a clever one. So this is to be a memorial, is it?"

Karl cleared his throat and waited until Lien looked him in the eye. Then he said softly, "I would be honored if you would let me help build it."

* * *

Late that evening near bedtime, Sam walked into the kitchen to get a glass of iced tea. Lien was seated at her usual place at the table, reading a book. Sam sat down across from her and smiled. "What are you reading?" he asked her in Vietnamese.

"*David Copperfield,*" she answered with a grin. "It sure is a long book."

"Were you able to show Karl the place?" Sam asked.

"Yes, sir," she said. "Karl had a lot of good ideas for the garden and said he would be honored to help me with it. Wasn't that nice of him?"

"Yes, it was. Is everything settled between you two?"

"Yes, Daddy. I think we understand each other now."

"I'm glad to hear that, sweetie, because I think that Karl is a good man. I believe that he always liked you but just wasn't aware of it."

"Huh?" Lien said, slightly puzzled.

"Never mind. I'm just glad you two have fixed it. You know, sweetheart, we all have a right to some respect, and the right not to be judged for the color of our skin or the country we were born in, but with that right comes the need for charity. There are always going to be people who won't like you because you are from Vietnam. The war will be a part of a lot of lives for a long time. Just be careful that you don't end up carrying a chip on your shoulder, going around and waiting for someone to say the wrong thing. You will end up being miserable, and it's no fun knowing that people are walking on eggshells around you, always afraid they are going to say something that offends. Do you savvy?"

Sam stood up and kissed his daughter on the forehead.

"Don't stay up too late."

"No, sir, I won't," she said with a smile, closing the book. "Thanks, Dad."

Fourteen

Mrs. Davison Comes to the Rescue

Amberley sat in the living room by herself, listening to the rain and the distant thunder. Everyone was gone except for Mary, who was singing under her breath in the kitchen. It was midafternoon, and Amberley thumbed through her book of poems, the gift Hank had brought on his last, and perhaps only, visit. She couldn't concentrate on the poetry, and she wished that Ma would come in and keep her company. Just then, she heard a knock at the back door and a familiar woman's voice speaking with her mother.

"Amber, see who's come to tea!" Mary said, carrying in a tray. There behind her, smiling a beaming smile, was Amberley's teacher, Mrs. Davison.

"Hello, honey. How are we feeling?" she asked, kissing Amberley on the cheek and seating herself next to her. "You certainly look well today."

Amberley smiled. Mrs. Davison was just what the doctor ordered. "I feel okay, but I'm just so weak. I sure have missed you and school."

"I know, dear. I have missed you too. I was hoping that you and Brenda could start college together this fall. Perhaps you still can."

Amberley, no longer smiling, looked into Mrs. Davison's face for a sign that she was jesting. But she and Ma were still smiling sincerely.

"Dear," Ma said, "Mrs. Davison has a wonderful idea, but I'll let her tell you about it."

Margaret Davison set down her teacup and leaned forward. "Amber, I have a niece who was just discharged from the army after eight years of service. She was a combat nurse in Vietnam several years ago and has served all over the world. I have invited her to stay with me until she can find a job. I asked her if she would be willing to tutor you this summer and set up an itinerary whereby you might meet the criteria to graduate. If you are diligent and willing, I believe you could have your diploma by the end of August. It would give her something to do, and I know you two will get on just famously. What do you say?"

This news was so unexpected that Amberley didn't know how to answer, but she was sure she could do it.

"Oh, Mrs. Davison, how wonderful! Yes! Yes, I would love that very much!" Then Amberley paused. "But Ma, can we afford it? I wouldn't want her to do it for charity."

"Now Amber, you leave that to your father and me and concentrate on graduating," Mary said.

"Then it's settled," said Margaret Davison. "I am expecting Beth this weekend, and she will contact you to let you know when she can start. I have determined what you will need to finish your senior year and graduate, and I will leave it to Beth to set it up. I know you will just adore her."

"And now, let's have some tea and cookies. Brenda made these fresh this morning," Mary said. Amberley took a sip from her cup and smiled. She would never be as smart and sophisticated as Hank—but she might just get a college education after all.

* * *

After breakfast on Saturday morning, Brenda took Amberley for a long drive along the dusty country roads. Amber was feeling spry after the good news from Mrs. Davison, and a brand-new feeling was beginning to sprout inside her: the feeling that things might just turn out after all.

After an hour or so of enjoying the beautiful countryside, the bright red Studebaker again pulled up to the edge of the porch steps. And for the first time since she'd left the hospital, Amberley was able to get out of the car and walk up the stairs by herself. As she turned to make her way to the kitchen door, there on the porch table was a vase filled with a dozen pink roses. On the floor next to the swing was a large cardboard box.

"Well, it looks like you have an admirer. Perhaps it's from Karl," Brenda said, teasing.

"Stop it!" Amberley said with a grin as she sat down and held one of the roses to her nose. She plucked the card from the vase and hurried to read it. Amberley smiled and quickly put it back into the envelope. "It's from Hank!"

"Is it a nice card?" Brenda asked. "What does it say?"

"Oh, you are nosy, Brenda! Here, read it for yourself," Amberley answered, handing her sister the envelope. Brenda read the card aloud:

> *I am sorry for making you so blue, so I sent you these. I remembered your favorite color,*
> *Hank.*

Amberley struggled to pick up the large box from the deck of the porch, but it was too heavy. Finally, with Brenda's help and a grunt, they set it on the table.

"Now for this mystery!" Brenda said as she went to the kitchen to get a knife. Soon the box was opened, and Amberley pulled back the flaps. "Well, I'll be . . ."

There in the box was a brand-new, top-of-the-line electric typewriter and several reams of typing paper. Amberley read the short note taped to the inside:

> *I thought this might make it easier for you to concentrate on your writing.*
> *Hank*

"He certainly is a character," Amberley said with a

smile, scratching her head. She didn't mention how much her heart warmed at the sight of the gift.

Fifteen
Beth

Monday morning was blustery: it had been storming off and on since midnight. The wind was wild in the trees, and the front and back yards of the house were strewn with branches and leaves. Black and gray clouds hung low, moving swiftly overhead, giving forth occasional gushing downpours of heavy rain from an almost tropic weather pattern. So dark was it outside that the porch light still burned brightly.

Amberley stood at the window in the kitchen and let her nose touch the glass. This was to be her first day of lessons with Beth, and she feared that the weather might keep her away. She knew that every day from now until the end of August would be precious. Until she held her diploma in her hand, college was still little more than a pipe dream.

Mary had invited Beth to come over early for dinner to give them all a chance to break the ice. Amberley tried to imagine what kind of person she was. Fresh from military service and a nurse, she had certainly seen a lot, and Amberley imagined that she must be intimidating. Her last name was Collins, and Amberley remembered how Miss Collins, now Mrs. Davison, had been when she'd first met her—hard as rocks and bitter. But Amberley was older now, and perhaps Beth was just the kind of person she needed to spur her on in her studies.

As the clock ticked closer to noon, Sam and Karl walked through the kitchen door, hanging their dripping raincoats on the rack along the wall.

"Well, the sun can peek its head out between the clouds anytime now," Sam said, wiping his face on a towel.

"Humidity and never-ending rain—reminds me of the jungle," Karl said. "At least here in the States there is a place to get dry."

Sam and Karl pulled out their chairs to sit at the table as Brenda and Grandma Andrews were setting the places.

"Remember now, boys, we're having a guest today for dinner," Grandma said. "Mrs. Davison's niece will be here shortly. Have some iced tea while you wait."

Suddenly, Lien came running down the stairs from her room to the kitchen, all in a flutter.

"She's here! She's here! Oh, what do we do?" she exclaimed, hurrying to pull back the curtain and look out the kitchen window.

"Lien, what has gotten into you?" Mary said sternly. "Beth is our guest! Now settle down and wash up for dinner."

Lien nodded and tried to calm her fluttering stomach. Amberley was not the only one anxious over Beth's coming. Lien had already contended with one old soldier who had spent time in the country of her birth, and now she would be meeting another. How would Beth react to her? Would she treat her as a normal American thirteen-year-old girl, or would Lien see that odious look she had first seen on Karl's face again?

Amberley watched as a small, bright yellow sports car with California license plates buzzed up the driveway and parked near the steps of the porch. The driver quickly emerged, and a clear plastic umbrella festooned with yellow daisies burst open. Its owner scurried up the steps to the door, closing the umbrella almost as quickly as she had opened it. Amberley hurried to let her in.

"Hello, folks," Beth said, forward and cheerful as if she were already well acquainted with everyone. Far from the stiff, formidable figure Amberley had imagined, Beth Collins was a short, petite woman with long black hair fixed in a ponytail and parted in the middle. She wore a blue, ankle-length cotton granny dress and a necklace of small turquoise stones. On her feet were leather sandals. Beth leaned her umbrella against the wall and stuck out her hand in Amberley's direction.

"You must be Amberley," she said, shaking her hand. "Aunt Maggie told me to be on the lookout for the red hair and freckles. I am looking forward to working with you. I'm sort of in between jobs right now, and unless I keep myself busy—I'll go absolutely nuts!"

"Pleased to meet you," Amberley said, pointing to a chair. "Won't you sit down to dinner?" *Letting Beth in is like letting in the wind!* Amberley thought.

As Beth sat down at her place, she noticed Lien seated across from her with her head hanging down. Reaching across the table and touching her chin, Beth slowly lifted the little girl's head until they made eye contact. "And who are you with the sweet little face? Won't you look at me?"

"Yes, ma'am," Lien said softly, trying to smile. "My name is Lien."

"Will you be my friend, Lien?" Beth asked. Then she spoke a few words in Vietnamese. Sam raised his eyebrows in surprise as Lien's smile lit up her face and she answered in kind.

The rest of the family and Jeb were introduced. "And this is Karl," Mary said. "He helps us run the farm."

Beth reached across the table and shook Karl's hand. "Hello, Karl," Beth said, squinting her eyes for a moment as she looked at him but saying nothing more.

After dinner, the men went back to their duties, and Amberley and Beth repaired to the living room to begin their lessons. Beth unlatched her narrow briefcase, took out a single sheet of paper, and handed it to Amberley.

"I've made an itinerary that will take us from today to the end of August. Aunt Maggie and I have discussed it and determined what we'll need to cover. If all goes well, I can even give you the date of your graduation. How about that?" Beth said with a smile.

"That's wonderful," Amberley said, inspired by Beth's manner and enthusiasm.

"I am most comfortable using a chalkboard, and your mother told me she had one I could use. Are you up to taking notes?"

Amberley nodded, almost overwhelmed. "Yes, ma'am."

"None of that now. My name is Beth. My mother was the only 'ma'am' in our family. Now, my methods are as follows: I will discuss the material we are to cover each day for a whole week, and on Friday after class, I will give you study guides that I have written covering the highlights of the various subjects. The following Monday, before we start our lessons for that week, I will give you a test on what we covered the previous week. It should be a breeze because the test questions will come directly from the study sheets. I don't believe in tricks. The tests are not long, just enough questions to determine whether you understand the material. If you listen to me all week and go over the study sheets on the weekend, you should ace the Monday-morning tests. Is that fair?"

"Yes," Amberley said.

Beth smiled. "Good. Then let's get started. Aunt Maggie tells me that you are particularly bright and have been studying right along on your own. Now, let us redeem the time, as the Bible says."

Sixteen
Fourth of July Picnic

It was near the end of June, and Amberley was doing well in her studies. Relieved of the burden of having to travel to school each day, she rarely got sick and could feel her strength returning. Beth, her tutor and now her friend, was so vivacious and fun to be with that the time went swiftly by. And she was a good teacher. Amberley was sure that September would find her enrolled in college.

Amberley also noticed that when Beth showed up each day, Karl would choose that particular time to say "Pardon me for interrupting!" and fill his canteen with ice water from the refrigerator. Beth would smile at him, and he would smile back, but nothing was ever said. *How do people ever manage to get together?* Amberley wondered.

After Beth departed one afternoon, Brenda asked her sister if she would like to go for a malted milk at the Sister Lakes drive-in. Happy for a chance to get out for a while, she consented, and soon they were driving down dusty County Line Road.

After the carhop brought out the tray and hung it on the edge of the window glass, Brenda spoke.

"Sis, Joe and I have come up with an idea, and we wondered what you thought of it. We want to have a picnic on the Fourth of July for just us kids, and maybe go to the fireworks later in Eau Claire. What do you think?"

"What do you mean by 'us kids'?" Amberley inquired.

"I mean Joe and me, you and Lien, Karl, and maybe Beth, if she'd like to come. All of the older folks are going to the Civil War reenactment in Lawton for the day."

"I think it's a wonderful idea, and I'm sure Beth would love to come. Where do you propose to have it?"

"At Joe's farm, of course. He's done so much work that it's become quite a place. Joe is planning on roasting a hog, and he thinks he may have some sweet corn ready to pick by the Fourth." Then Brenda paused. "I was thinking of inviting Hank."

Amberley had not thought of Hank. She was still not sure where they stood, and perhaps he wouldn't be comfortable at a simple picnic in the country. Besides, she was still a bit peeved over his father. Her own mixed feelings confused her. Perhaps she expected Hank to come fawning back with apologies.

Amberley answered carefully. "I'll have to think on that, sis. Hank's very busy and may have to work and . . ."

"Amber!" Brenda interrupted. "Are you balking at this because you're afraid of what Hank may think, or is it something else?"

Amberley was surprised at Brenda's bluntness. "Not a bit of it! Down deep, I don't think Hank is that way. It's just that I was sort of rough on him the last time he was here, and except for the roses and the typewriter he sent me and a vague letter I received yesterday, I'm not sure where we are."

Brenda took a sip from her straw, looking straight ahead. "Amber, at the risk of getting you upset with me, I'm going to say something. If you keep making Hank jump through hoops, you're going to lose him—as a friend and whatever else. If he gets the impression that you are going to make him pay for every misunderstanding, he will start to avoid you."

"Is that what you think I'm doing?" Amberley said, bristling at her sister's candor.

Brenda turned and looked her straight in the eye. "Amber, Hank is lonely and tired, and from what you told me, he's not getting support and approval from his father. I don't think you're doing anything on purpose to hurt him, but the effects are still the same. I don't know where you think this relationship with Hank is going, but I can assure you that he won't hang on forever. If he thinks that what you are doing is, well, childish and the way you always operate, he will seek someone else's friendship. And why shouldn't he? The sea is full of fish that are less challenging. He comes to you for rest, an oasis from his harsh, weary world. If you make him work too hard for it, he'll stop coming."

"Then what am I supposed to do?" Amberley demanded, the frustration showing in her voice. Brenda had struck a nerve.

"Have you tried to see this from his point of view? Have you ever sat down and supported him with letters and cards? He can't help how his father is, and he's not responsible for what he says. Hank is teetering on the fence of decision here, and if you really care for him as you say you do, then you need to stop feeling sorry for yourself and be an encouragement to him."

Brenda's words couldn't have hit Amberley harder. The sisters sat in silence for several minutes. Finally, Brenda started the engine of the Studebaker and turned on her lights to signal the carhop that they were ready to leave.

"Not yet, sis," Amberley said, putting her hand on Brenda's arm. "You're right. I have been sulking and making Hank pay for his father. I didn't think I was that kind of person, but I am. Thanks for reminding me. I know it wasn't easy."

"Oh, you know me. I usually get around to saying something profound eventually," Brenda said with a smile, backing out of the drive-in to return home. "Uh, so I can invite Hank?"

Amberley smiled. "Sure," she said.

The Big Farm in Old Sodus

* * *

The morning of the Fourth was warm and humid, and the sky looked like rain. Karl had finished the milking, and he waved at the Producer's Creamery truck as it left to go to the next farm down the road. At midmorning, he stopped for a break and walked back to the deserted kitchen for a cup of coffee and a doughnut. The so-called "older folks" had left already for the village of Lawton in Van Buren County to spend the day at the Civil War festivities. The three sisters had gone to Joe's to help set up for the picnic, which left Karl all alone. He had declined an invitation from Brenda, saying that he was too busy—but now he wished he had accepted.

Returning to the henhouse, Karl began to collect the eggs that would have to be washed, put into cartons, and stored in the cooler. The air was thick and pungent. He felt the sweat running down his face as he checked the nests and methodically pushed aside each hen to feel for the fresh-laid eggs. As he wiped his face with his sleeve, he heard the door squeak open behind him.

"I hear you're too busy to join our little shindig. Is there anything I can do to help?" Karl turned. There, dressed in a stylish green dress with a paisley pattern, was Beth.

Karl was surprised but didn't let it show. "I've got it handled. Besides, I don't want you to get your clothes dirty. And this isn't a good place to walk around in sandals," Karl said, nodding his head in the direction of her feet.

"Ooh! You ranger types are all alike. Too proud to have anyone help you," Beth said firmly, promptly picking up a basket and collecting eggs beside Karl as if she had done it all her life.

Karl said nothing as he worked his way down the row of nests. "Who told you I was a ranger?" he said finally.

Beth smiled. "I know you don't remember me, but I remember you. I helped hold you down once, while the doctor dug a chunk of white phosphorous out of your leg. You were lucky. Afterward, I took care of you until they could fly you out of there. I'm Army Nurse Captain Beth Collins, or at least I was. And you are Staff Sergeant Karl McNee, or at least you were. How's that for a memory?"

Karl shook his head. "Impressive."

"How's the leg?" she asked.

"Fine, except when a storm system moves through. I hardly ever think about it. You must have done a good job taking care of me."

"I cared for a lot of guys over there, but even though the war has been over for several years, I never forgot you. Perhaps it was the way you tried so hard to mask your pain and your feelings. You know, sort of like you're doing now," Beth said, with only a faint smile this time.

"What do you mean?" Karl asked, shifting uncomfortably.

"Like turning down the invitation to the picnic today,

even though you really wanted to go. You were the same way at that field hospital in Vietnam."

Karl stopped and for the first time, looked directly into Beth's eyes. "How could you know that? And what about Vietnam?"

"You were in such terrible pain, but you always tried to hide it. The doctor ordered morphine, but you refused to let us give it to you. You just lay there moaning and sweating and grinding your teeth, like a little Boy Scout trying so hard to be brave."

Karl tilted his head back as he looked at Beth. Long forgotten thoughts and feelings and smells of those days came rushing back. Everything she had said was absolutely true. Karl unconsciously felt the spot on his leg.

"You didn't know it, but when you finally passed out from the pain, I slipped in and gave you your shot. I'll never forget the sounds you made as the pain released its grip and you were finally able to rest. I came in every day, even on my time off, to make sure you took that shot. I couldn't stand to see you suffer. Not when there was something I could do about it."

Karl was without words as he stared into the eyes of the most remarkable person he had ever met. "How could you remember all of that?" he said softly, almost under his breath.

"I guess it's just the way my brain is wired. Those particular memories are so vivid," Beth answered, reaching under a nervous hen. "And now, let's finish gathering these eggs. We should be just in time for the picnic."

"Beth?" Karl began after a long pause. But Beth shook her head, putting her finger to her lips. "Not now," she said. "We'll talk more about it later."

* * *

It was nearing twilight, and everyone was seated on the porch, talking about going to the fireworks in Eau Claire. Joe and Brenda chatted with Beth and Karl. Lien had fallen asleep in the hammock in the yard, and Amberley sat alone, watching the dusty road for Hank's car that did not come.

"I'd better wake up little sister before the mosquitoes carry her away," she said, stirring from her chair. It had not been a happy day for her, and evidently Hank was detained at the hospital again. Or at least, that was the excuse he would give.

"I think we can all fit into the Studebaker," Brenda said. "Karl and Beth can sit in the backseat with Amber, and Lien can sit between Joe and me."

Just then, a pair of headlights came down the dusty road and turned into Joe's driveway. Amberley was on her feet before she knew what she was doing. It was Hank. He was very late, but he was there. Everyone stopped talking as Amberley walked out to his car to meet him. Brenda paid particular attention, not sure what her sister would do.

The Big Farm in Old Sodus

Hank closed the car door behind him. "I suppose you don't want to see me. I have an excuse from my doctor, if that matters," he said with a weak smile and a pathetic attempt at humor.

Amberley paused and without emotion, reached out to take Hank by the hand. "You don't have to explain; I'm just glad you're here."

Seventeen
Jeb Goes Another Round

During the weeks since he had come to work on the Bridges farm, Karl had often noticed Jeb seated in his padded Adirondack chair under the large maple in the backyard. Day after day he sat expressionless, watching Karl as he worked. Karl deduced that the old man was feeling useless, like an old workhorse banished to the back pasture. It was pretty obvious that Jeb had been feeling better with proper rest and medication and longed to have some part of the daily operations of the farm again.

On one particularly warm and overcast day, Karl noticed Jeb in his usual place and walked over to speak with him. "Can I sit down and join you in a cup of coffee, Jeb?" he asked, helping himself from the carafe Mary had brought out.

"Sure, son. Sit down an' take a load off," Jeb answered, pleased that the young man had stopped by.

"Kind of warm today, Jeb. I still can't get over how warm and humid it can get up here in Michigan. But I shouldn't be surprised; it was the same on the farm in Wisconsin when I was a boy."

Jeb nodded and stared off in the distance, looking over the hazy fields. Karl cleared his throat. "Jeb? I was wondering if, from time to time, I might be free to ask your advice on different things. You have worked here for a long time, and I feel I could benefit from your knowledge and experience."

Jeb was surprised. "Anytime, young feller! Yer obliged to anything I can hep ya with."

"And," Karl continued, "maybe sometime you might give me a hand on some projects? I know you are retired, and I wouldn't want to put you to work again, but sometimes a guy just needs a hand from somebody who knows what he's doing."

Jeb smiled and took a gulp of coffee. "Sure, sure, I would be happy to give ya a hand anytime ya say."

"Thanks, Jeb," Karl said, setting down his cup. "I would be crazy not to take advantage of what you know. And anytime you have some advice for me, just say the word and don't worry about hurting my feelings. Well, it's back to work. Talk to you later."

Karl returned to his chores, giving a wave at Jeb as he went.

"What a nice kid," Jeb said with a grin, suddenly feeling ten years younger.

* * *

    Several days later, after a particularly tedious day of work, the family sat together at the supper table. Karl helped himself to several slices of roast turkey, cornbread dressing, mashed potatoes, and giblet gravy. It tasted wonderful, and after another helping, he sat back in his chair.

    "Sam, I've noticed that the engine on the pressure washer is losing compression. I checked the cylinder, and it's time for an overhaul. I could probably do it Saturday morning after the milking if I could have Jeb's help."

    Mary and the girls stopped eating and looked up at Sam. The room grew silent. "Karl, Jeb here is retired," Sam said gravely, not looking up from his plate.

    "Oh, that's too bad. I sure could have used his assistance, but if he's retired . . ." Karl continued.

    "He's paid his dues, and I want him to take it easy from here on out," Sam said firmly, now looking up at Karl.

    "Never mind, Sam," Jeb blurted out. "If the boy needs muh help, then he needs it. Karl? Would ya like me to go inta town and get the parts so'z we can have a go at it on Saturday?"

    Sam put down his fork. "Now, Jeb—I don't want you working anymore—"

    Jeb interrupted, indignantly sticking his jaw into the air. "Sam, iff'n ya won't let me do what I can do, ya might as well shoot me and put me in that hole up on the orchard hill!"

"But Jeb," Sam began again, "I'm just thinking of you."

"Iff'n I'm retired, then I'm ta do whatever ah wants. Then leave me be an' let me hep Karl."

Mary, Grandma Andrews, and the girls all looked down at their plates, almost shaking the table in an effort to suppress their laughter. Jeb had spoken and shown them all that like an old boxer, he still had a few good rounds left in him.

Sam looked around the table. Everyone was grinning at him, including Karl. "All right, Jeb," Sam said with a sheepish smile. "I know when I'm licked. Have it your way."

Eighteen
Surprises Come in Threes

It was a hot Monday afternoon near the middle of August as Amberley waited on the porch swing for Beth to come. Today was a test day, and she carefully read over her notes, confident that she would do a fine job. If all went well, it would only be two more weeks before she would have her diploma.

Even though the generous scholarship from Mrs. Holloway would allow her to attend college anywhere she chose, Amberley had decided to enroll in a local community college with Brenda to start. Brenda wanted to be near Joe, and Amberley had the same idea about Hank. She would be able to take preparatory classes there, leaving her future open for whatever she wanted to do. Brenda had already enrolled, but Amberley was at an impasse until she had her diploma in hand.

Beth pulled into the driveway at her usual time, her bright yellow car freshly washed and waxed. Amberley smiled, suspecting that Karl had something to do with that.

As Beth walked up onto the porch, Amberley poured her a glass of iced tea.

"Hey, kiddo," Beth said. "You ready for your test?"

"I sure am. Can we do our lessons out here today? It is so warm inside the house."

"I was going to suggest that. My, that tea tastes good," Beth said, setting down her dripping glass on a wooden coaster. She pulled the stapled test out of her briefcase. "Today's test will be a little longer. I've included a few questions from the material we covered earlier in the summer. I want to see what you remember."

"Oh dear!" Amberley said. "I hope I do well. I wasn't prepared for that."

Beth smiled. "You will do just fine. Are you ready to get started?"

Amberley put the test on her clipboard and settled back in the swing. There were almost twice as many questions as usual, but she didn't mind. Beth was fair, and so was Mrs. Davison.

She smiled as she noticed Karl walking across the yard, presumably to get his usual canteen of ice water. She smiled again when she saw Beth tell him to wait in the shade by her car as she went into the house to retrieve it for him. Although nothing had been said, it was obvious that there was a growing understanding between the two of them, and the sweetness of it made Amberley feel happy inside.

Soon, Amberley finished the last test question and set

the clipboard down on the table. She took a sip from her glass and handed the test to Beth, who had just returned from her chat with Karl. "It was a hard one," Amberley said. "I hope I did well."

"I'm sure you did. Go stretch your legs, Amber, while I grade this for you."

Amberley stepped off the porch and breathed in the hot air. Even though she enjoyed working with Beth, she would be glad when it was all over. It had been a long year for her. Her terrible sickness, the long recuperation, and finding her way with Hank had taken everything out of her. She had imagined last year that she would have a normal end to her high school career and a leisurely summer vacation to rest up before starting a new life as a college student. Instead, she had grown up overnight. Frankly, she felt as if she had been robbed of part of her childhood.

"Amber?" Beth called to her. "You can come back now."

Amberley retook her seat next to Beth and examined her graded test. In red, "100%" was written at the top of the page. She smiled. If she could keep this up, she would soon be a college student, and that would make up for all of the bad things that had come her way. At least, she hoped it would.

"Oh, Beth! I'm so happy and so close—I can just feel it!"

Beth reached into her briefcase and pulled out a red grade book. "Aunt Maggie gave me this so I could officially record your grades. Now, taking my pen in hand, I will write in today's test score and that is that."

"I am ready for today's lesson, Beth, whenever you are," Amberley said, inserting a white legal pad under the clamp of her clipboard.

"I have a much better idea, Amber. How about . . ." Beth paused and pulled out a manila folder, which she handed to Amberley, ". . . we have a graduation ceremony instead?"

Amberley held the folder and narrowed her eyes, trying to comprehend.

"Go ahead, open it!"

Amberley opened the folder. There inside was her official high school diploma.

Amberley's mouth dropped open, and her eyes grew wide. "Are you serious? For me?"

"Yes," Beth said. "For you. As of this minute, you are an official graduate of River High School in Sodus Township."

"But—we've not done our lessons!"

Beth smiled. "Aunt Maggie figured you had done enough. You have faithfully tried to keep up with your studies, even when you were still in the hospital. You knew the material, and after a few tests, she was sure you were ready. She wanted you to be free to enroll in college right away and not be rushed."

Amberley stood up and hugged Beth with all her might. "Oh, thank you, Beth! And I must thank Mrs. Davison too! Oh, she is so kind, so very kind! And Beth, I have a confession to make. When I first heard about you, I was so intimidated. I didn't know what to expect. I thought you might be hard and mean. Then that first stormy day when you came here and I saw your yellow sports car with California plates and the way you dressed with your sandals, I . . . I thought you must be a hippie!"

Beth burst into laughter and gave Amberley a peck on the forehead. "I guess I do operate on a different wavelength from most people, but that's the first time I was ever accused of being a hippie. I love it!"

Amberley couldn't wait until evening so she could surprise her family with her diploma. She would go out the very next day and enroll in college. Then, on her way back home, she would purchase a bundle of flowers and take them over to Mrs. Davison, her dear, sweet teacher from the old days.

* * *

Amberley had been so overwhelmed by the anxieties of her studies and college that now, with everything all settled, she did not quite know what to do with herself. She tried to keep busy and exhibit enough character to do some writing each day, but her spirit was not willing. She missed Hank and wondered if matters would ever work themselves out.

Late morning on an overcast day, Amberley decided to

walk out to the mailbox, hoping to find one of Hank's wearily written letters from his late hours at the hospital. As she rounded the corner, she almost ran into Karl. "Sorry, Amber, I got the mail for you. Nothing from Hank," he said.

Amberley smiled. "How did you . . . never mind," she said, taking the stack of mail from his hand. Karl said nothing more but walked away to return to work.

"Karl?" she said, as he turned again to face her. "You miss Beth coming over each day, don't you?"

Karl smiled, but nothing came out.

"You don't have to say it. I know a lovesick puppy when I see one," Amberley chuckled. "She is quite a gal, isn't she?"

Karl only grinned and waved. It was obvious that he had feelings for Beth, but where it would all lead, only the Lord knew for sure.

Seating herself on the porch, Amberley shuffled through the stack of mail until she came to a large envelope addressed to her. Hurrying to open it, she pulled out the contents: it was a magazine and an envelope with her name on it. Still not comprehending, she opened the envelope. Inside was a check for one hundred dollars, payable to Amberley M. Bridges. Then it finally sank in. It was a royalty check for the article she had sent in to the children's magazine. She was a published author!

Amberley quickly skimmed through the magazine, page after page, until she found her story. There it was.

There was her name on the byline. She ran her fingers over it as if she were reading Braille. Then she held it to her nose to smell the ink. All that had happened to her that year, and now this. She held the magazine to her breast and burst into tears. *Oh, thank You, dear Lord. Oh, thank You!*

* * *

Hank's next day off was coming up soon, and he had made plans to spend it with Amberley. She had planned a picnic near the St. Joseph River at the edge of the hollow. It would be a warm day but cool in the shade of the trees near the flowing water.

She could hardly wait. She planned on having fried chicken (perhaps so she could tease Hank again), fresh-baked bread and butter, potato salad, deviled eggs, and key lime pie. Hank had told her in his last letter that he had something important to tell her, but she couldn't imagine what.

Finally, it was Thursday, just after the noon whistle from the Sodus Fire Department sounded, and Amberley waited patiently on the porch swing. Karl had hitched up Gray to the buggy and parked it in the shade near the porch for her. Although Hank had gotten off his shift at six o'clock that morning, she had asked him to please take a long nap before coming over for dinner. Amberley wanted him rested and not associating her with his lack of sleep and weariness.

Amberley stood up and stared down the long driveway to the road. She glanced at her watch and then back down the road again. *A little more and the chicken will be cold!* she thought. Then she heard an engine race and saw Hank's dark blue BMW fishtail down the drive in a great cloud of dust. Hank opened the door of his car and got out. Amberley was surprised. He was still wearing a blue smock from the hospital.

"Amber, I'm so sorry, and so full of excuses! I just got out of there. They grabbed me on my way out the door this morning to assist in an emergency surgery. I just washed up, threw on a clean smock, and rushed out the door to get here."

Amberley looked at him. His handsome blue eyes more closely resembled red-hot coals. He needed a shave and was so tired that he was having trouble speaking coherently.

"Do you mean you have been working over twenty-eight hours straight?" she asked.

"Well, closer to thirty, but who's counting? Is there any food left? I haven't eaten in almost as long."

"Oh, Hank! You can't keep this up. Doctor or no, you're going to get sick. How can they expect you to function like this?" Amberley asked, moisture welling up in her eyes. Apparently, she did care deeply. Hank noticed her tears.

"Actually, Amber, in the medical world, this is considered a privilege. I just have to get used to it, that's all. Now about that food?"

"I'm so sorry, Hank. I had planned a wonderful picnic by the river . . . but please sit down and eat something."

Hank sat down on the porch swing as Amberley dished him up a plate. He inhaled the food and asked for seconds. "Sorry to be a pig, but this is so good. Did you make this yourself?"

"Yes, I did, and I'm glad you like it," she said graciously. Amberley was tempted to make the comment that "country girls all know how to cook" but decided that it wasn't the right time. Hank was working hard to get through his residency, and she was beginning to understand that this would be the dominating part of his life for several more years.

"Would you like some more, Hank?" she asked. "More pie?"

"No thanks. I'm stuffed," he said, holding his stomach. "But I wouldn't mind taking a drive through those woods you keep telling me about. I don't know anything about horses, though."

"I can drive, Hank, if you're sure you're up to it."

"Sure, sure—just point me in the right direction."

Amberley and Hank were soon driving down the bumpy path through the hollow to the river. "I hope the mosquitoes aren't too bad. If the breeze isn't blowing they might eat us alive," Amberley said, trying to keep the conversation light. "Hank, did you say you wanted to tell me something today?"

"What? Oh, yeah," he said, reaching into his pocket. "This is for you." Hank handed her an envelope. It was folded in half and wrinkled. "Sorry," he said. "I stuffed it in my pocket on the way out the door."

Amberley held on to it until they came to the river. Gray put his head down and drank from the edge of a cool spring that was bubbling out of the ground near the shore. Amberley looked at Hank and then opened the envelope with her thumbnail. It was a very fine quality of stationary, written in a beautiful feminine hand:

> *My dear Amberley,*
>
> *I have not had the privilege yet of meeting you, but I am looking forward to it. Hank has described you in such sweet and glowing terms that I feel as if I know you already. I was so sorry to hear about your recent illness and am glad that the Lord of Providence has chosen to heal you.*
>
> *It would be, therefore, an extreme honor if you would agree to spend the Thanksgiving holiday with us at our home in Chicago. If you would come the day before and stay through the weekend, we would love the opportunity to get to know you and render our hospitality. Please let us know of your decision.*
>
> *Sincerely,*
> *Marjorie Wheeler*

P.S. I would also like to extend my invitation to your sister Lien. We are most anxious to meet her, and she would be a companion for you during your stay among strangers.

Amberley reread the letter again and set it down in her lap. How unexpected—and how strange. The letter appeared to be sincere, but having inherited some of her father's suspicious nature, she couldn't help thinking that the invitation was just a fact-finding mission on the part of Hank's father under the ruse of a holiday visit. And why had they invited Lien?

Amberley's first inclination was to decline. Besides, she couldn't imagine that her father and mother would approve. She would be at Craig Wheeler's mercy, and who knew what he might ask her? She was sure that Hank's father would like nothing better than to provide evidence to his son that she was everything he claimed she was. Amberley had heard that lawyers were sneaky and could trick you into saying things that weren't true. She had to find a way out of this graciously.

"Hank?" she said, turning to speak with him. But it was no use. Hank, in his exhaustion and with a stomach full of her good cooking, had curled up and fallen into a deep sleep. She looked at him, and her heart nearly melted. He was like a tired little boy who had played hard all day and now couldn't keep his eyes open.

Whether or not the Lord had laid the notion upon her heart she could not tell, but she vowed that moment to do everything she could to help him get through his residency. If this was what Hank wanted and had to do, she would support him, no matter how their relationship progressed. She would at least be a good friend. If spending Thanksgiving in Chicago with Hank's parents was part of that, she would do it. As for Lien coming along, that would be up to her parents and, of course, Lien herself.

Nineteen
Sam Wants to Know

It was early afternoon, and Amberley sat at her blue wicker desk in the corner of her room alone. She and Brenda had attended their first day of classes at the community college, and now it was time to study and do homework. Amberley was tired despite having done very little, which told her that she still had a long way to recuperate before she was completely back to normal.

As she sat at her desk, gazing out the big window, she thought how nice it would be to have a cup of hot tea. She stood up to go to the kitchen but soon realized that if she went downstairs to get it, she might be too tired and shaky to come back up. *Just so many trips up and down these stairs a day for me,* she thought to herself, smiling. *Perhaps Lien would fetch me a cup.*

Amberley stood at the top of the stairs and called out for her little sister, hoping she would be in the kitchen. Finally, after she'd called twice, Lien's voice answered back, agreeing to bring her a cup of tea.

Amberley sat back down, and soon she heard footsteps coming up the stairs. She heard a knock and turned to thank Lien when, to her surprise, there stood her father, holding a steaming cup in his hand.

"Here's your tea, Amber," he said, setting the hot cup on the desktop in front of her.

"Oh, Dad, you didn't have to do this. You're too busy to be waiting on me."

"Well, I enjoyed bringing it up to you, and besides, I thought we might have a little chat. It seems that everything has been sort of a whirlwind these last few months, and I wanted to see how you were doing," Sam said, seating himself in the chair in the corner.

"Sure, Dad, fire away!" she said. "What would you like to know?"

Sam sat back in the chair and looked around the room. "You have a nice room here," he said. "It has to be twice the size of your old room in Sodus."

"Yes, I think it is. It's nice to have plenty of room to keep your things," Amberley said.

Sam smiled, nodding his head. "I was just curious—how are things going with Hank Wheeler? I know that he has been writing you and has visited a few times. What exactly is going on between you two?"

"Well," she began slowly, "we are good friends, and we got sort of close while I was in the hospital."

"How do you feel about him? Is this thing getting serious?"

Amberley smiled and thought carefully before she answered. She wasn't about to deceive her father, but she wasn't sure what to tell him. "I . . . I think a lot of Hank. At first I wasn't sure, but now I believe I have feelings for him."

"Are you sure this isn't just a crush on the doctor who helped save your life?" Sam asked seriously.

"Maybe at first it was, but now I do care for him. He is such a nice guy, hardworking and dedicated to becoming a practicing doctor. I *am* grateful for all he did for me, and I admire him for that. Perhaps that's what first drew me to him. We were both lonely and thrust together all those months in the hospital. Then one day, something happened —I can't explain it, but I fell for him." Amberley blushed a little, disappointed at her inability to explain her feelings.

"I see. How does he feel about you? Has he said anything to make you believe that he feels the same way?" Sam asked, putting his hand on his chin.

"Well, Hank is not the easiest person to nail down. It's like pulling teeth to get him to tell me things—but he told me that he cared for me. And I could tell that something else was bothering him, and he finally leveled with me. That's how I found out about his father."

Sam leaned forward in his chair. "What does his father have to do with this?"

"Hank's father is a wealthy attorney, and he hired a

private investigator to find out what he's been doing while living here in Michigan. That's how he found out about Hank's friendship with me. Mr. Wheeler thinks I'm too young for him and suspects that my interests in his son are only material."

"What does Hank say about all of this?" Sam asked, obviously uncomfortable with hearing his daughter portrayed in such a way.

"Hank told me that he doesn't care what his father thinks. Mr. Wheeler confronted him about me, and they had a heated discussion, ending in a veiled threat to cut Hank out of his will," Amberley said, watching the clouded expression on her father's face.

"Apparently," Amberley continued, "this is not the first time something like this has happened. Hank told me that his older brother, Richard, who is an attorney living in California, has cut all ties with his family in Chicago after a similar row. It seems that Richard took a Vietnamese bride while he was stationed over there, and his father blew his top. Even though the woman is beautiful and sophisticated and was the daughter of a high-ranking government official, it wasn't enough. Richard and his wife have several children—twins, I think."

"Doesn't he care to see his grandkids?" Sam asked.

"Hank told me that his father refers to them as 'half-castes' and refuses to have anything to do with them. I don't think that Mr. Wheeler is a very nice man," Amberley said, happy to be able to freely confide in her father.

"He is very bitter," Sam said. "But what about you? Do you think you are too young for Hank?"

"I don't feel that I am. I am eighteen-and-a-half, and Hank is twenty-six. And . . . well, after all that I have gone through this last year, I feel much older than eighteen."

"Well," Sam said, standing up from his chair, "I just wanted to make sure you weren't going too fast and that you had your eyes wide open. If this thing becomes serious, I think you are more than able to deal with Mr. Wheeler." Then Sam chuckled. "Your Grandpa Andrews wasn't terribly thrilled when your mother told him that I had proposed to her. And I suppose he was right about a few things back in those days."

"Daddy?" Amberley said. "Before you go, I have something to ask you."

Sam sat back down. "Go ahead, sweetie."

"Hank's mother wrote me a letter and asked that I spend Thanksgiving with them in Chicago," Amberley said, handing him the envelope. "I want you to read it."

Sam opened the letter and read it carefully. "I can understand why she might want you to visit—but Lien?"

"I am a little perplexed about that too. Why Lien and not Brenda?"

"I would venture," Sam began, folding the letter and handing it back to his daughter, "that Mrs. Wheeler has it in her mind to use Lien to soften her husband up so that he might accept his daughter-in-law and grandkids. If Lien can charm his heart of stone, he might see his error."

"I'll bet you're right, Dad. But what do you think? Would you and Ma be willing to let Lien come with me to keep me company?"

Sam thought long and hard. "I need to discuss this with your mother. I think you are able to handle Wheeler just fine, but I'm not willing to subject Lien to a man who has already shown himself to be hostile and opinionated. I am going to need some convincing that she will be all right, perhaps from Hank himself."

"I understand. And I appreciate you coming up to speak with me. I feel so much better."

Sam smiled, his fingers interlaced, and looked at the floor. "You know that Mr. Wheeler may make it rough on you. If he really believes you are all of those things he said, he might attempt to show you up in front of Hank. Can you take it?"

Amberley paused to gather her response. "I think so. I am not worried about what a bitter old man thinks. And I want to size up the situation for myself. I want Hank to be sure that I am worth all of this trouble. Besides, I do want to meet his mother. Hank says that I remind him of her."

"Okay, I'll speak with your mother. You are old enough now to start making these kinds of decisions for yourself," Sam said, rising from his chair and kissing her on the cheek. "One more question. May I assume that Hank is a Christian and that you wouldn't be seeing him if he wasn't? It doesn't seem like he comes from a Christian home."

"Hank's roommate in medical school led him to Christ. Hank showed me the Scofield Bible that he got as a gift. He wrote the date he got saved on the inside cover. He hasn't been baptized yet, and he asked me once if Pastor Mitchell might do it. I guess I learned a lot about Hank during those long weeks in the hospital. He's not a great Bible scholar, but his heart is tender and I know he loves the Lord."

* * *

Later that evening, Sam and Mary sat together in the kitchen. It was bedtime, and everyone else had already gone upstairs. Mary reached over and took the bottle of honey from its place on the table, unscrewed the lid, and poured some into her cup of tea.

"I don't like it, Sam. The nerve of that man, thinking and saying those things about our daughter! For him to think that our dear, sweet girl's intentions are mercenary! And now she will be going right into his clutches?"

"I feel the same way, Mary. Craig Wheeler is a hard man. But Amberley is not a child anymore, and she is old enough to make her own decisions. She is bound to make them, with or without our approval."

Mary turned and looked wide-eyed at Sam. "But how can we let her go to that place with that . . . man? And the gall of Mrs. Wheeler—asking us to let Lien go along!"

"We're not 'letting' Amberley do anything, Mary. She is going on her own, and all she asks is our understanding. That shows that she does care about what we think. And Mrs. Wheeler is right about one thing: Lien would be good company for Amber. They may just learn some things about human nature—good and bad."

Mary sat back in her chair and took a deep breath. "And they will be leaving the day before and staying through the weekend? I'm not crazy about her driving all alone, both ways, with Hank. I trust my daughter, Sam, but it just doesn't look right."

"Well, Amber will be with Lien, so she won't be alone, and Hank is a gentleman as far as I can tell. I think this trip will show our daughter exactly what she needs to know about Hank and his family. And it may accomplish something else. Unless Craig Wheeler's heart is made completely of stone, Lien may lead him to think again about his daughter-in-law and grandkids. Remember, Mary, how wrong we were about Mrs. Holloway from King's Landing. Everybody is a little strange, depending upon one's point of view. Give Mrs. Wheeler a chance before you write her off completely. And before we let Lien go anywhere, we are going to have a long discussion with Hank. It will be up to him to convince us that his father will behave himself."

"But Sam, what about our Thanksgiving here? Our holiday is falling apart!" Mary said mournfully.

"Not really, Mary. There will be Brenda, Joe and his mother, Jeb, Karl and Beth, the Davisons, Grandma Andrews, and us," Sam said, counting on his fingers. "That's a houseful. It's Thanksgiving, Mary. The Wheelers have all of the money in the world to make them happy. Now let our daughters show them what the Bridges have to be thankful for."

Twenty
The Harvest Supper

Bright sunlight topped the horizon in the eastern sky and began burning away the heavy fog that had risen during the cool, still night. As the daybreak moved on, the occasional sound of a pickup truck or tractor bumping up and down Park Road could be heard.

Joe was done with his morning chores, and he took his coffee to the front porch and sat down. His mother was busy in the kitchen making breakfast, and he could smell the sage from the frying sausage. It was a chilly morning, but Joe loved to sit out on the porch where he had sat with his father many times over the years. It comforted him and helped him when he needed to think.

As the moisture slowly dissipated and the sun shone brightly in a blue sky, Joe finished his breakfast and put on his hat to resume his chores. He stopped on the porch and leaned against one of the posts, folding his arms in thought. He had been wrestling for several days with a personal matter, and now those thoughts suddenly turned to resolve.

Quickly disappearing back into the house to change from his work clothes into something better suited for the public, he started up his old black pickup truck and let the engine warm. A steady blast of bluish-white smoke from the tailpipe told him that his engine was starting to burn oil, and a slight knock in the crankcase meant that it wasn't long for this world. *How can I ask Brenda to live like this?* he pondered.

He couldn't quite answer that question, but he knew if he was to have any future with her, he would have to keep moving ahead.

Joe set out toward the city. When he arrived, he parked his truck along the main street. He was in no hurry to get out, and for a few moments, he just peered over the top of his steering wheel. Then, with a sudden jerk of the door handle, he exited the truck and fed the parking meter at the curb. Joe put his hands in his pockets and turned to walk down the sidewalk, looking and feeling every bit of a rube.

Stopping in front of a small jewelry store, he stood outside, gazing into the show window. Taking a deep breath and grasping the handle, he walked inside and let his eyes focus. He had never been in such a place as this before, and his timidity showed on his face and in his manners.

"May I help you, sir?" a young lady behind the counter asked with a smile. Joe didn't know what to do with his hands, so he quickly shoved them into his pockets again. He approached the glass counter, leaned forward, and stared at the trays of rings in front of him. He had no idea what he was looking for and even less idea where to begin.

"Looking for something in particular?" the clerk asked.

"What kind of a ring would a girl like?" Joe blurted out awkwardly.

The young clerk bit her lip to keep from laughing. "Is this an engagement ring?"

"Is that the same as a wedding ring?" Joe asked.

The clerk smiled. "No, an engagement ring is what you give your girlfriend when you ask her to marry you. You purchase the wedding ring at the same time, but she doesn't get that until she says 'I do.'"

Joe gave the clerk a sheepish, embarrassed smile.

"And what size is your lady's finger?" the clerk asked again.

Joe had not thought of that, and he marveled at how the simple, sweet notion of giving your girl a ring could turn into such a complex series of unanswerable questions. The clerk took several sets of rings out of the display case and showed them to Joe, but he was overwhelmed. Then he asked the fateful question: "How much do these run?"

The answer almost knocked him off his feet. Joe had known that a ring would be expensive, but these seemed unimaginably far beyond his financial reach. Excusing himself and tipping his hat to the further amusement of the clerk, Joe said he would be back and quickly departed the store—miserable, bewildered, and wondering how he could have been so foolish. He was sure that Brenda would marry him because they had an understanding, but it wasn't right that she wouldn't have a proper ring. But the truck engine would not last much longer without an overhaul, and the truth was that he did not make enough money farming to take care of his widowed mother, let alone a wife.

"The dream was a good one while it lasted," Joe said out loud as he started up his old truck and headed back to Shanghai in a cloud of blue smoke, hoping the police would not stop him.

* * *

It was the last Saturday of October, the day of the big harvest supper, and everyone looked forward to it with delight. The large storage building between the big barn and the chicken house was made of thick, heavy stone blocks and was filled with the smells and delights of the summer's bounty. Bushels of red and golden apples kept the cider press running with cold, sugary-sweet juice. A brown mountain of russet potatoes was piled high on the cold concrete floor next to acorn and butternut squashes and pumpkins. Red mesh bags of Spanish onions hung along the walls next to gunnysacks of popcorn ears, waiting to be shelled, popped, and eaten with melted butter before a winter's fire. The hogs had been butchered, filling the smokehouse with hanging hams and sausages and causing the savory scent of the escaping apple wood fires to waft through and around the breathless air of the farm.

Sam and Karl had decided to experiment with making cheese that year, using Grandpa and Grandma Andrews's old recipe. This was not unfamiliar territory to Karl, who, being from Wisconsin, had helped his father and grandfather make cheese as a young boy. Several dozen rings of cheddar cheese, coated in wax, sat curing on the shelves in the cooler.

The kitchen had been ablaze since long before dawn. Grandma Andrews had been baking dusty loaves of white, rye, oatmeal, apricot, and tomato breads, and the occupied cooling racks on the counters and table were evidence of it. Pork and beef roasts and juicy hams had been slow-roasting through the early morning hours in their rich, thick juices.

Mary had made several large casseroles: one of onion-and-sage cornbread stuffing, another of green beans flavored with thick homemade mushroom soup and crispy fried onions, another of scalloped potatoes in a creamy white sauce with chunks of boiled ham and tiny pearled onions. She had also made two cast-iron Dutch ovens full of baked beans, flavored with dark molasses, brown sugar, and slices of salt pork that had been slow-baking since the night before. There was a large kettle of corn chowder with crab meat and another of tomato soup made with cream and just a hint of celery.

Brenda had again shown her talent for making desserts.

Her apple, peach, and pumpkin pies crowded the long white shelf in the walk-in pantry, fragrant and cleverly decorated. Amberley showed what she could do by making several pecan pies and cheesecakes with cherry sauce.

Karl and Joe busied themselves making a fire pit in the corner of the backyard for the bonfire later that evening. They neatly stacked a pile of logs nearby, cut from old plum and apple trees. Joe and Karl had become good friends and enjoyed each other's company. Karl admired Joe for his genuineness and considered him a rustic version of himself.

As the men set up chairs and benches in a semicircle around the pit, trying their best to contemplate the direction the smoke would blow, Karl spoke. "Joe, I noticed that your pickup is burning a little oil. Have you thought about what you're going to do about it?"

Joe was surprised. The problem had been eating at him, but he didn't think that anyone else had noticed it. "No, I guess I'll jus' run it till it falls apart," he said thoughtfully.

"Well, the reason I'm asking is that I know of a wrecked Ford pickup. The engine only has about thirty thousand on it, and the farmer is going to have it hauled off to the scrap yard. He told me I could have the engine for nothing. All I have to do is yank it out and it's mine. I was thinking that we could pull it out next Saturday and swap it for yours. It would only take a couple of hours, and your truck would run like it's brand-new."

Joe looked at Karl, vacillating between relief and worry.

It would be such a load off his mind if this could be done, but . . . "That sounds great, Karl, but I have no money for it."

Karl's ever-present smile grew wider. "Apparently you weren't listening to me, Joe. It's free-e-e! All we have to do is add our sweat to it. Consider it a wedding present, if you must, from me to you. And if it bothers you that much, you can buy the pizza."

Joe looked at Karl and then said, "Who said anything 'bout a wedding?"

Karl grinned. "Come on, Joe. Who do you think you're kidding? You love that girl, and sooner or later you will marry her. And she's crazy about you too. Besides, nothing much stays a secret on a farm. Now let's get these tables set up before the rest of the people get here. But first, maybe the ladies will pity us and let us sample a plate of that good cookin'. I'm starved!" Karl put his hand on Joe's shoulder and led him toward the house while his friend kept trying to let it all sink in.

* * *

It was past midnight, and all of the guests had gone home. Brenda and Amberley had said their good-byes to Joe and Hank, and Sam and Mary had gone up to bed. Outside, the slight breeze that had blown all day had ceased, and a frost was beginning to form on the leaves and grass.

Seated side by side in front of the dying fire were Karl and Beth. Karl had tucked a heavy quilt about her and scooted his chair up a little closer.

"Beth, could I get you some more coffee or hot chocolate?" he asked.

"My goodness, no! I probably won't be able to sleep now as it is," she answered. "And I probably should go. You have to get up in a few hours to do the milking."

Karl ducked his eyes. "I like having you around, Beth, so please don't go on my account."

"That sounds nice right now, but you will hate me when the rooster crows and you can't open your eyes," Beth chuckled.

Karl watched the glowing embers in the fire pit and the puffs of smoke as they rose straight up into the air like tiny, spectral imps, slowly drifting away. He was anxious to speak to Beth and knew that every moment he waited made it more unlikely that he would. Finally, taking a deep breath, Karl reached over and took Beth's hand. She was not surprised. Nor did she look up.

"I keep thinking that this is the very hand that wiped my sweaty brow in that jungle hospital and gave me those shots to ease my pain," Karl said with some emotion. "I wish this hand belonged to me. All I have to offer you, Beth, is a lot of nerve for asking you to even consider me. I milk cows and wash eggs for a living. Not exactly something you can brag about to your friends."

Beth squeezed his hand and then held it with both of hers. "Karl, we both served our country over there. What we are now is not necessarily what we will be. We're both getting back on our feet. I have been working part-time at Berrien General, and you like your job here with the Bridges family, don't you?"

"Sure I do, but where would we live? That little cabin is hardly big enough for one person, let alone two," Karl said with some frustration.

"Or maybe three or four or five or . . ." Beth said, laughing.

Karl grinned. "You know what I mean, Beth. I do love you and want you to be my wife, but it just wouldn't be fair to you."

"So what happened to my airborne ranger? Is that what you were trained to do, let obstacles get in your way and stop you?"

Beth turned and looked into Karl's eyes. "You said you wished that this hand belonged to you. If you truly want it, then it's yours," she said. "So now that's settled. We can work out the logistics later. I've lived in smaller places than that cabin and so have you. It will all work out, Karl, I promise you."

Beth stood up and kissed him. "I have to go, and you have an early morning. Mrs. Bridges invited me over for supper tomorrow, and we can talk more about it then. Is it a date?"

Karl smiled and put his arm around Beth as he walked her to her car. "I'll make a home for us somehow," he said.

"I know you will, Karl, and I'll make a home for you. You know, I think I first loved you when I took care of you in that field hospital in Vietnam." She reached up to kiss him good-bye and then quickly got into her car to leave. "I am so amazed that God would bring us back together again. He does things like that, you know, for those He loves."

Karl put his hand on his cheek and waved as Beth negotiated the long, dark driveway to the road. He had never met anyone like her—and now she would be his and he would be hers.

How am I ever going to get any sleep tonight? he thought as he walked across the dark yard to the humble cabin that had once belonged to Jeb and his wife and now, most likely, would belong to him and Beth.

Twenty-One
Thanksgiving in the Windy City

After a hurried midmorning lunch, Amberley, Lien, and Hank set out on their journey to the suburbs of Chicago to spend Thanksgiving with the Wheelers. Hank was anxious to leave as soon as possible to get a jump on the heavy holiday traffic they would certainly encounter as the afternoon wore on. Thousands of cars, bumper to bumper, would be pouring in and out of the great city like ants returning to their nests.

Amberley and Lien were quiet at first. What should have been an exciting adventure to a place they had never been was instead a somber experience. Neither of the girls had ever been to Chicago, and except for a few short trips to the big city of South Bend, just below the state line in Indiana, Amberley had never been very far away from her home in Sodus.

Hank was quiet too. He had spent an evening with Sam and Mary Bridges, assuring them that Thanksgiving with his family would be a delight. But privately, he wondered if this whole thing was a bad idea. He knew that his mother was a class act and would go out of her way to befriend the two sisters, but how would his father respond? If he thought of the girls' visit as one last-ditch effort to preserve life as he knew it . . . well, he wasn't sure. Hank thought about Richard and his Vietnamese wife and children. His father did not even try to hide his contempt for them. How would he react when he saw Lien, let alone Amberley? He was sure of one thing, he would not allow his father to be unkind to the girls, and if he had to, he would follow his brother's lead and sever all connections with his family in Chicago. His father's threat to disinherit him did not concern him—if he had to, he would go it alone.

Stopping for a short break near Gary, Indiana, to get gas, Hank decided to go through the Chicago Loop so the sisters could see the Sears Tower, the tallest building in the world. Amberley was amazed at the sight of the massive skyscraper, and facing the traffic, concrete, steel, and congestion, she made a subconscious decision that she would never live in such a place as this. It frightened her, and she could not image what circumstances or sacrifices would force her to change her mind.

Lien sat with her hands folded in her lap, listening to Hank and Amberley's conversation in the front seat, but was too shy to add anything to it. She too was amazed at the junglelike city of concrete and asphalt—a different kind of jungle than she had known as a little girl. Her mind drifted back to the time she visited the big city of Grand Rapids and how it had intimidated her. She too would not willingly leave the security of her country home in Sodus anytime soon.

"Hank, where do all of these people come from? Is it like this where your parents live too?" Amberley asked.

Hank smiled. "Well, it seems that the people who live in the city work in the suburbs, and the people who live in the suburbs work in the city. Twice a day they cross paths, going to and from work. I'm glad I never had to do it."

"It's all so intimidating!" Amberley said. "I feel like a child learning to walk. Perhaps your father is right. I do feel like a country hick, and right now, I can't think of anything else I would rather be."

Hank smiled and glanced at the pretty red-haired girl with freckles seated beside him. He loved her but had not uttered those words to her yet. It wouldn't be fair. He wanted Amberley to be free to experience the weekend with his family, to form her own opinions and conclusions. If she decided it was not what she wanted, then she would be free to back away without the added pressure of a romance. But deep in Hank's heart, he loved her very much and would be willing to live with her anywhere—including Sodus, if need be.

"I envy you, Amber, and your whole family," Hank said finally, and with deep sincerity. "You are richer than my family has ever been or ever will be."

Amberley laid her head against the window glass as the warm sunlight made her sleepy. She had only known one rich person, and that was Mrs. Holloway. Although very wealthy, she had lived a frugal, reclusive life and only spent what she needed to live. The Wheelers, on the other hand, flaunted their wealth and power. What should she expect when she arrived at their home? Perhaps there would be a great stone mansion with a hundred rooms, and dozens of servants working day and night to heed and satisfy every whim of their master and his lady. Amberley imagined a wooden dinner table, fifty feet long, with high-backed chairs, set with fine linen, silver, and gold. She could see a small army of butlers and maids going about their duties with fear and trembling, knowing that one small indiscretion would send them out of the house to the unemployment line without a recommendation.

As the darkness began to settle in, Lien and Amberley were again impressed by the heavy traffic in the Chicagoland area. Cars and trucks, stopping and going, bumper to bumper, and bright headlights as far as the eye could see, like strings of pearls with no place to go and no purpose for their existence.

Finally, after several long hours in Hank's car, they exited the highway and were soon surrounded by the lush, gardenlike suburbs of the north side. Hank turned down a winding driveway that was almost as long as the long drive of the big farm. Stopping his car under the large, wide portico at the front of the house, with its white pillars and ancient vines of ivy, Hank spoke. "Well, this is it, such as it is. Someone will be here shortly to help us with the luggage."

Instantly, the double-doored front entrance opened, and several servants came out and began to gather the sisters' suitcases and baggage, carrying them inside. Hank opened the doors for Lien and Amberley, taking them each by the hand and helping them out of the car and to the door. As they walked into the large foyer, Lien remembered how intimidated she was years before when, as a little girl, she had entered the huge federal building in Grand Rapids. She didn't have her beloved Sam to hold her and comfort her now. She had to act grown-up and keep her chagrin to herself.

As the sisters stood in the entrance beside Hank, several women in maid's uniforms quickly took their coats and wraps, bidding them to follow them into the next room. The room was very large and bright, the walls painted crème and the high ceiling ornate and white like the icing on a wedding cake. Standing there, alone and with a beaming smile, was a beautiful older woman holding her arms out to embrace her son. Hank walked over and gave her a long hug and kiss before introducing her to the sisters.

"Mother, this is Amberley."

Marjorie Wheeler hugged Amberley and then, holding her by the shoulders at arm's length, looked her up and down as if she were examining a work of art. "How lovely you are, my dear! Hank has told me so much about you. Please be at ease and enjoy yourself this weekend. My hope is that we will get to know each other very well."

"Yes, ma'am," Amberley said. "That is also my desire." She hoped her words sounded sincere. Amberley was suspicious of Hank's mother, but she didn't want to be. She wanted to believe that Mrs. Wheeler was like Hank, genuine and sincere. She didn't want to think that she might be working in concert with her husband, to show her up and ultimately destroy her in Hank's eyes.

"And this is Lien," Hank said, placing his hand on the younger girl's shoulder.

Mrs. Wheeler's eyes began to sparkle as she studied Lien's face. She pulled Lien to her and hugged her long and hard. "There now," she said, taking the two sisters by the hand and leading them into the drawing room, "let's sit down and visit while supper is being prepared. Was the traffic heavy?"

"Yes, ma'am," Amberley answered. "I have never seen the like before. It almost took my breath away."

"I know," Marjorie said. "I'll bet you wonder how people can live like this. I still do, and I have lived here all my life. Sometimes I wish I was in the country where I could look out my window and see the mountains and lots of green grass."

"Perhaps someday you might come to Sodus and see the big farm and the hollow. It is so very beautiful in the springtime," Amberley said.

"My dear," Marjorie said, "you said that as if you were seeing it now. I should like to visit it someday. Perhaps I will."

Amberley smiled at her. Despite her suspicions, she could not help but like this woman. She was charming and seemed to be down-to-earth, though only time would tell.

"And you, my dear," Marjorie said, addressing Lien, who sat small and silent next to her on the couch, "what was your impression of the city?"

I've got to be a big girl, now, Lien thought. "It was frightening, ma'am. I didn't like it very much."

Marjorie Wheeler laughed out loud. "I love your honesty, dear, and you are right. I don't like it much either. Have you ever seen Lake Michigan? This weekend we can drive over to the shore and let you see our freshwater ocean."

"We have seen it before, ma'am," Amberley said. "We only live a few miles from it back home." Then Amberley caught herself. *I hope she doesn't think I was being saucy!*

Mrs. Wheeler's eyes sparkled. "Then we must all be good friends, for we have only Lake Michigan between us."

A tall, thin butler announced that supper was on. Amberley looked at him. He wasn't anything like Theodore, Mrs. Holloway's butler—the tall, stiff giant from King's Landing. This man smiled and even teased the sisters as he seated them at the big table in the dining room. Amberley watched Mrs. Wheeler for signs that she was put off by her butler's informality, but she seemed amused at his humor. Even the uniformed maids who waited on them seemed at ease and amiable. So far, nothing Amberley had seen was as she expected. The servants all seemed happy and contented.

"Will Father be along soon?" Hank asked as he unfolded his napkin and placed it on his lap.

"He is still in court—a very big case, you know. He told us not to wait for him and that he would be along as soon as he could."

Hank asked the blessing as everyone bowed their heads. The butler and maids, standing to the side, folded their hands in front of them and closed their eyes. Lien bowed her head but peeked out of one eye. She looked around at Mrs. Wheeler and the wonderfully spread table. She wondered what exotic foods were under the shiny silver lids of the serving trays. Perhaps it was turkey. Rich people might have turkey every day—or was it pheasant? Maybe it was some French dish prepared by a real chef with fancy sauces and a fancy name. Lien understood a little French, as did many people in Vietnam. And what kind of desserts would be served after such a meal?

"Amen," she heard Hank say, and Lien quickly closed her eye and lifted her head with everyone else as if she had been a good girl during prayer.

"Now, Tom," Mrs. Wheeler said to the butler, "you may

serve our guests first. These ladies looked famished."

Tom? Amberley thought to herself. *Tom is not a butler's name!*

Tom picked up one of the silver platters with a tall domed lid and brought it first to where Amberley sat. Lifting the lid with a smile, he asked, "Will you serve yourself?"

Amberley tried to hide her surprise. Instead of a succulent turkey or fancy beef roast, there were several dozen hamburgers in their buns. She picked up the tongs from the edge of the tray and placed one of the delicious-looking sandwiches on her plate.

"Oh, take another one," Tom said. "They are not very big." Close behind Tom was a maid, holding a large platter of crispy, hot French fries draining on several sheets of parchment paper. The maid placed a large stack of the fried potatoes on Amberley's plate next to the hamburgers. As the butler and maid finished serving everyone, another maid set bottles of ketchup and mustard on the table within everyone's reach. Lien took a sip of her drink from a beautiful crystal glass, furnished with a straw. *Root beer!* she thought with a big grin.

"I hope the food is to your liking, ladies. It was a toss-up between hamburgers and hot dogs, so I let Cook decide," Marjorie said with a beaming smile. "Perhaps this weekend we can have hot dogs. Chicago makes the best hot dogs in the world, you know."

"Yes, ma'am," Amberley said. "This is fine." *Perhaps Mrs. Wheeler thinks we are not sophisticated enough for anything but hamburgers and hot dogs,* she thought. She looked over at her sister for a reaction, but Lien had already taken a bite out of her hamburger and was busily munching on her fries. As Amberley began to sample her food, she looked around the table. Marjorie and Hank certainly seemed to be enjoying themselves. Could she have been wrong about the Wheelers? How did Craig Wheeler, the man Hank had described, fit into this scene? Or perhaps they were buttering her up so she would let down her guard, making it easier for Mr. Wheeler to cross-examine her later on.

Amberley bit off the end of one of her French fries. She remembered how suspicious they had all been of Mrs. Holloway, the rich widow from King's Landing, and how wrong they had been in the end. *I will give Mrs. Wheeler the benefit of the doubt—and Mr. Wheeler too!* she thought. *If God is in this thing, then it will all iron itself out. I keep forgetting that God does things for the benefit of people on both sides of the fence. Perhaps God wants to help the Wheelers too.*

* * *

The mantel clock had sounded ten times, and Craig Wheeler, all alone in the drawing room, laid down his newspaper and stared at the slowly dying embers before him. The fire had all but burned itself out, causing the flickers and shadows in the room to fade. It had been a long day in court, and even though he had been the victor, he had lost the ability to savor it as he had in the days of his youth. It was just a job to him now. He had achieved all of those things in life that are supposed to make a man happy—position, respect, and wealth. And yet he was left feeling empty and forlorn.

Craig Wheeler had willingly followed the wishes and footsteps of his father, as had his father before him. Was it too much to ask that his sons do the same? But they had not shared his dreams and were not at all intimidated by his threats of disinheritance. All he had accomplished was to tear his family apart.

Wheeler heard a sound behind him and turned his head, expecting to see one of the servants ready to replenish his cup of tea or stoke up the fire. He was surprised to see Lien standing there in her pajamas and robe, rubbing her eyes.

"And who might you be?" Wheeler growled, expressionless and fingering the corner of his mustache.

Lien blinked at him like a tiny little owl perched on a high branch. "I am Lien. I came with my sister Amberley for Thanksgiving dinner, remember?"

"Why aren't you in bed, little girl? Are you ill?"

"No, sir, I just can't sleep in a strange bed. I thought I would watch your fire for a while if you don't mind."

Wheeler patted the cushion next to him with his hand, and Lien sat down, folding her hands in her lap. The two sat together in silence, staring into the fireplace, when Mr. Wheeler spoke. "Would a glass of warm milk help you to sleep?"

"It might, sir. You never can tell," Lien answered. "Will you have one too?"

"I was thinking about it," he answered. "I was also thinking about having a piece of apple pie. They say that sugar makes you sleepy. Would you have some with me?"

"Yes, sir," she answered. "I like apple pie."

Craig Wheeler stood up and pulled on the long cord hanging from the ceiling next to the fireplace. Soon, a young woman in a maid's uniform came into the room and stood silently before them. "Two glasses of warm milk and two pieces of apple pie for me and my guest here."

The servant vanished as quickly as she had come, and Wheeler looked at his young visitor. "How long have you lived in Michigan, child?"

"I think it's been about five years or so. I was adopted by the Bridges family when my folks died."

"Did your adopted father bring you home from Vietnam when he was in the army?" Wheeler asked.

"No, sir. My parents died here, and I went to live with Dad and—I mean, Sam and Mary—because Sam could speak my language. He was a Green Beret, you know." Then Lien told him the whole long story about her parents' terrible deaths in Hipps Hollow and the particulars of her short life in Sodus. So engrossed was Mr. Wheeler with Lien's narrative that, when brought back to reality, he chuckled. "Well, it seems that while our spirits were engaged in conversation, our bodies consumed the pie and milk while we weren't looking."

It was true. The milk and pie were gone, and Lien scarcely remembering eating them. Mr. Wheeler smiled at his guest. He found himself strangely drawn to her and touched by her story.

"And you say the soldiers from Vietnam left you on the airplane that was on fire? How dreadful that must have been for you."

"Yes, sir, and if those two Green Berets dressed as firemen hadn't saved me, I would have been killed. They were friends of my dad, Sam Bridges," Lien said proudly.

"He sounds like a remarkable man. I must meet him someday," Craig Wheeler said with an uncharacteristic smile.

"Oh, I wish you to meet him, sir. He is very like you—strong and kind. My Sam would have known that I needed a glass of milk and pie. He has always loved me too."

Wheeler bit his lip and faced the fire. After a few moments of silence, Lien yawned and scooted up next to Craig Wheeler, laying her head against his chest. Soon she was fast asleep. Wheeler cautiously put his arm around her, unsure of whether or not he should. Deep in thought, he watched the little girl as she breathed and thought to himself, *This could be my granddaughter.*

After the last ember of what had been a roaring fire extinguished itself, Craig Wheeler carefully picked up Lien in his arms and carried her to her bed, tucking her in. As he stood there momentarily, watching her sleep, he was suddenly struck by the guilt of all of the hours and minutes wasted—time he could have been spending with his own grandchildren. Bending down, he kissed her forehead and softly closed the door behind him.

* * *

The next morning, Amberley and Lien dressed quickly and walked down the long semi-spiral staircase to breakfast. Amberley was nervous at the prospect of meeting Craig Wheeler for the first time, but Lien didn't seem in the least bothered. She was smiling and cheerful.

Tom the butler greeted them as they walked across the room and directed them to their places at the table. Hank and Marjorie Wheeler were already seated. Mr. Wheeler's chair at the head of the long table sat ominous and empty like a throne. Amberley and Lien took their seats and waited quietly, their hands folded in their laps, trying to smile.

At long last, a soft cough was heard coming down a long hallway which connected to the dining room—and there at last was Craig Wheeler, tall, thin, and wearing a suit. He did not smile or look at anyone directly but walked to his place at the head of the table. Amberley could feel her skin crawl, and her nervousness almost made her nauseous. Then, to everyone's surprise, Craig Wheeler stopped at Lien's chair, bent down, and kissed her on the cheek. "Good morning, my dear."

Lien smiled and reached up to hold his hand. "Good morning to you, sir. Did the pie make you sleepy after all?"

"It sure did," he said. "And I look forward to another piece after Thanksgiving dinner. Will you join me then?"

"I sure will, sir, and with a glass of milk?" Craig Wheeler smiled and nodded.

As Wheeler took his seat, everyone at the table except Lien stared at him with their mouths open. But no one said a word about it, including Mr. Wheeler and Lien. It was their little secret.

Craig Wheeler's eyes fixed on the nervous red-headed girl sitting beside Lien. He shook out his napkin and placed it across his lap. "And so, this must be Amberley. Was the drive up a pleasant one?"

Amberley paused for a moment and then said, "Uh, why, yes."

"Now, now," Wheeler said. "You can tell the truth. Driving through the Chicago Loop at rush hour before a major holiday? It was miserable, wasn't it?"

Amberley smiled and blushed. "It *was* miserable, sir. I

was just trying to be polite."

"Well," Wheeler said with a wink and a smile at Lien, "we all know that it's best to be honest, don't we, and to be ourselves?"

Lien said nothing but smiled and winked back, leaving everyone at the table, including the servants, to wonder what had happened to Craig Wheeler.

Twenty-Two
A Wonderful Gift

Jeb sat alone in his place at the kitchen table next to the stove. He stirred his coffee to the rhythm of the noisy wall clock and noted how good the heat made his bones feel. He had never thought much about the holidays, especially Christmas. The day he lost his wife and son had left a lifelong void in his heart, and the holidays were only for those privileged to have families.

This would be the end of his first year retired and living in the big house. He considered the decorations, and for the first time, began to feel as if he truly might be one of the family. Taking another sip of coffee, he heard someone coming into the kitchen and turned to look.

"Jeb Sanders, are you sitting out here alone?" a voice asked. It was Grandma Andrews.

"Jest enjoyin' the stove, ma'am."

"Are you hungry, Jeb? Can I fix you something?"

"No, ma'am. I'm jes' fine."

Marion Andrews poured herself a glass of fresh buttermilk from the refrigerator and stirred in a dash of salt and pepper. She pulled out a chair and sat next to Jeb at the table.

"Jeb, I've wanted to speak to you for quite a spell. You know how I am. I can be crusty and ornery at times, and I have been that way to you. I want you to know that I'm sincerely glad that Sam retired you and brought you into the house. I would have done it sooner, Jeb, but it wouldn't have been fitting—you and me being alone in the house together. But there's something I've always wanted to say."

Marion Andrews paused and cleared her throat. "Jeb, I've never forgiven myself for not being there for you when Abi was sick. When I think about that night and your little boy . . ."

Jeb hung his head and smiled. "Miss Marion, that was a long, long time ago. It wuzn't yer fault—never was. Don't try ta carry burdens that have already bin carried. You folks have been good to ol' Jeb."

Then Jeb sat up straight and cleared his throat.

"Ma'am, I would like ta talk to you 'bout somethin', iff'n ya don't mind."

"What is it, Jeb?" she asked, setting down her glass.

"Miss Marion, when ya put it in yer will that ya giv'd me sixty acres of land, did ya mean it?"

She blinked. "What a strange thing to ask, Jeb! Of course I meant it. It's yours. Mr. Andrews and I discussed it before he died, and he wanted you to have it. You know how much he thought of you and Abigail."

"Supposin' I wuz ta go first, what's ta become of the land?"

Marion Andrews paused, wondering where Jeb was going with this one. "What *do* you want done with the land, Jeb?"

Jeb smiled and held his cup with both hands. "Now Miss Marion, you know that ol' Jeb has no use for that land, never did, but I wants to ask yer favor in a very 'portant matter, an' I wants ya ta explain it all ta Sam an' Mary. Here's what I wants ta do . . ."

* * *

"There!" Mary said, licking the stamp and pressing it onto the envelope with her thumb. "They will probably decline the offer, but I can at least say that I made the effort. If you think about it, why would rich folks want to spend Christmas with us in the country, anyhow?"

"Well," Sam said, "you never can tell what people are thinking. A person can be alone in a crowded room and a rich man miserable amidst his gold and silver. Just perhaps, Mr. Wheeler, hard old barnacle that he is, might be hankering for a change. Let's see what happens."

Amberley sat at the kitchen table, listening to her parents talk. She took another thoughtful sip from her cup of tea. Christmas was just two weeks away, and the notion to invite Hank's parents had been a sudden one. Amberley was sure they would not come, especially when Ma had upped the ante by inviting Hank's brother Richard, his wife, and their twins from California. Perhaps the last-minute nature of things was good in that it didn't give either party time to brood. This would be the best and perhaps the only opportunity for the Wheelers to make amends with their estranged son. The holidays sometimes softened men's hearts and worked a kind of magic.

Amberley wondered if the Wheelers would have any inkling of the wonderful Christmas gift her parents were offering them—a golden chance to make it all right.

* * *

Mai Lee Wheeler sat on the patio of the rustic townhouse in the suburbs of San Francisco, watching her children play. A gentle breeze was blowing through the fronds of the palm trees that grew along the fence. It was a beautiful day, and Richard was to be home early to take them all out to supper.

Mai Lee sipped her cup of green tea as she sat in contemplation, tapping an envelope against the table with her other hand. It was an invitation from the Bridges family in Sodus to come for Christmas—with the Wheelers. She did not know what Richard's reaction would be. The truth was that Mai Lee had never met her father-in-law, Craig Wheeler. She regarded him as the very embodiment of wickedness, and it grieved her that Richard should suffer because he had married an Asian wife. It bothered her most that this man, wealthy beyond what he could spend in several lifetimes, should have so little regard for the two sweet children who busied themselves in play before her. Richard wanted nothing to do with his father, and she could almost predict his reactions to this invitation. Nevertheless, she would show him the letter after dinner and let him decide.

* * *

The snow began to fall gently all across Chicagoland from a weather system that had first invaded from Alberta, then moved through Montana, the Dakotas, Minnesota, and Wisconsin. It was expected to yield more than a foot and move slowly, lingering on through Christmas and New Year's Eve.

Craig Wheeler stood at the window of his large drawing room with his hands behind him, gazing up the long driveway that wound through his estate. The old barrister was nervous, an emotion that was uncharacteristic and strange to one who was so accustomed to being master of his circumstances, sometimes making the stomachs of prosecutors churn when he graced their courtrooms.

Marjorie Wheeler, his faithful and patient wife, stood beside him and held his arm. She turned around and looked at the beautiful tree that nearly reached the tall ceiling of the room and the few presents that did not come close to filling the space provided for them.

The long table in the dining room was set with the best china and silver, candles were lit and glowing, and garlands of holly and pine had been put on display to best advantage. Everything had been carefully prepared for a Christmas that might never come. The servants had long been dismissed to bed, and the couple was left all alone.

"Craig, what is it, dear?" Marjorie Wheeler asked. "You are so quiet this evening. Is your mind on work?"

Craig smiled at his wife. "I was just thinking of something my father said to me when he was dying. 'Craig,' he said, 'money is not flesh and blood and never will be.' I never understood what he meant until tonight."

"I don't understand, dear. Why would he say such a thing?"

Craig turned. "Don't you see, Margie? Father lived a long life, struggling to grab every dollar he could. He was the best at what he did and made our family very wealthy, but he died a miserable man. He had sought out the dollar but had neglected the important things in life—people! He was trying to warn me not to follow in his footsteps . . . and I missed it."

Craig and his wife sat down together on the couch in front of the crackling fire.

"My enemies fear me, and I was always proud of that.

My clients respect me for what I can do for them, but they do not love me or even like me. I have spent my life worrying about the firm, my legacy, and passing on my wealth to my children, to the extent that I haven't been a good father. Richard hates me, and Hank only tolerates me. I have a daughter-in-law and two grandchildren I have never met. What kind of monster does that make me, Margie?" Craig said, shaking his head.

Marjorie opened her mouth to speak but said nothing, fearful of how she might answer such a question.

Then Craig looked into her eyes. "Margie, let's go to Michigan! Let's accept the invitation from the Bridges and spend Christmas there. I am a miserable old man, but I would rather not die like one. If Hank is bound to have this girl, Amberley, then let us get to know her and her family. There is something about this place called Sodus, and I want to know more of it. I know it's late, but if you will phone them right now and tell them to expect us, I will call the office and tell them I'm taking some time off."

Marjorie blinked her surprise and smiled. "Oh, Craig! I will do that right away—this instant! It will make Hank so happy, and you will never know how happy it has made me." Still smiling, she kissed him on the cheek.

"And I need to tell the chauffeur to have the car ready right after breakfast," Craig exclaimed. "We have a long day of Christmas shopping ahead of us!"

Twenty-Three
A Sweet Interlude

It was the Sunday morning before Christmas, and life in the big farmhouse began to stir. It was a damp cold outside, and the steel-gray sky was randomly spitting particles of graupel snow that closely resembled soap powder on a washday. Breakfast was made as usual but not so heavy as it was on workdays, since dinner on Sundays was more elaborate with a pork roast, mashed potatoes and gravy, homemade bread, and a vegetable casserole.

Sam and Karl came in the back door from the milking, brushing the pellets of snow from their clothes. They paused to warm their hands over the woodstove and then sat down to hot biscuits and gravy. The girls all came down the stairs in unison, dressed for church, and took their seats around the big table.

"Where's Jeb?" Sam asked as he took a sip of hot coffee.

"He was up late last night. He said he couldn't sleep, so I'm sure he is running late," Mary answered as she pulled out her chair. "Go ahead and get started on breakfast. I'll check on him in a minute."

Christmas was just a few days away, and it would be a special day this year—even more than usual. Hank's parents would be coming, and his brother and family from California. Joe and his mother would be there too, along with Karl and Beth. There was so much to do, and Mary wanted it to be just right. Deep inside, she tried not to fret over the fact that no matter what she did, the success of this Christmas didn't depend on her. It seemed that this year, their merry Christmas was dependent directly upon Craig Wheeler and what he would do when he got there.

"I'll check on Jeb," Amberley said, scooting her chair back. "He'll be late for services if he isn't careful."

The conversation at the table continued to buzz as Amberley softly knocked on Jeb's bedroom door just off the big kitchen. There was no answer, so she slowly opened it a crack and peeked in.

"Jeb? Are you awake?" she said, peering into the semidarkness of the room. Snapping on the light switch, Amberley could see that Jeb was still sleeping. She smiled at the old man who was obviously tuckered out from staying up late and from life in general.

"Jeb?" she said softly, shaking his arm—and then recoiled.

"Daddy?" she shouted loudly and took a step back. Sam came rushing into the room and put his hand on the side of the old man's neck. After a moment, he pressed his lips together and looked into his daughter's eyes. "He's gone, sweetie. Jeb's taken the high road this morning and gone on to be with Abigail and his little boy and . . . the Lord Jesus."

Sam walked back to the kitchen, paused, and then spoke soberly. "Everyone come in here and say good-bye to this dear old man."

Slowly, the family gathered around the bed. At first they just looked upon the face of the man who had been a fixture on the big farm for so many years. His expression showed that he was at peace with his Savior. Slowly, the women began to weep, and even Karl wiped a tear from the corner of his eye.

Though Jeb was always humble and contrite and had never intruded into anyone's life, he was a blessed entity on the farm—like an old wall clock or a knickknack shelf. He would be missed, and there were many days of tears ahead for his adopted family, who were sadly left behind on earth to deal with life.

* * *

Amberley sat at her wicker desk all alone a few hours after noon. Jeb's funeral had been that morning, and she had just returned from his burial up on the orchard hill. It was sad but not so sad—Jeb was at last freed from his physical maladies and reunited with the tiny family that had gone on ahead of him so very long ago.

Amberley opened up one of her books of poems and read "Death of the Hired Man" by Robert Frost. She had always liked the line:

> Home is the place where, when you have to go there,
> They have to take you in.

Amberley hoped that Jeb had felt happy and at home here as much as he could. Besides his wife and child, the big farm was all he had. It had bothered her sometimes that Jeb never seemed to feel good enough and was so painfully aware of his perceived station in life. Perhaps they could have done better at making him feel of value instead of allowing him to go to seed over the years.

Now Jeb was at rest, and they had to carry on with very little time to mourn. Christmas was indeed coming like a freight train, and they only had time to pause for a brief, sweet interlude and then move on.

* * *

Christmas Eve morning was hazy and overcast, and the high-flying cirrus clouds were the color of fresh cream. It had not snowed in several days, but deep snow was everywhere, and Karl was up early, plowing out a small parking lot for the impending guests.

There would be a host of people to feed over the next

few days, and the kitchen was as busy as any small factory, with baking and roasting beginning well before dawn. Grandma Andrews had supervised the preparation of the two largest rooms for Hank's parents and for his brother Richard and his wife. Richard's two children would stay with Lien in her room—that is, if everyone decided to come.

Amberley wondered how Mr. Wheeler's first meeting with his Vietnamese daughter-in-law and grandchildren would fare. They were scheduled to fly into the airport at South Bend and drive up to Sodus together. Would Craig Wheeler have the elegance to bury the hatchet and make amends for the terrible rift he had caused in his family? Amberley remembered Thanksgiving and how kind he had been to her and Lien. Surely he had given some indications that he was willing and capable of changing, but only time would tell. Richard Wheeler had been hurt deeply by his father—would he be willing to forgive and meet him halfway? This could be the beginning of something wonderful or an irreparable disaster. Hank had decided to meet them at the airport too, just in case he needed to referee.

It was midmorning, and as all of the work and preparation seemed to be caught up, Amberley stole away to her room to change her clothes. As she washed up and put on a nice dress, Brenda came into the room and sat down on the edge of her bed.

"Amber, can I speak with you for a few minutes before everyone gets here?"

"Why sure, sis," Amber said, pulling a brush through her hair.

Brenda looked down at the floor for a moment and then spoke. "If things progress the way they have, it looks like you and I will both be formally engaged one day soon. I remember the first time I met you in school, when we were little girls, and how badly I treated you. I remember how you loved me and accepted me as your sister from the very beginning."

Amberley seated herself across from her sister and thought back to those days when she first came into their lives. Brenda was an angry and bitter girl, hating a world that seemed to hate her first. Amberley looked at her soft, delicate hands and remembered when they were a bully's hands—dry and calloused like her heart. But Christ came into her life and changed all that. Now she was truly a lovely young woman with a sweet, gentle personality. *How quickly our childhood together has passed.* Amberley sighed.

Brenda paused and then continued. "You and I have had a few bumps along the way, but we have always been close. I would give anything if that would never change."

"But Brenda, it *will* never change. How could it?" Amberley said.

"Let me finish," Brenda said, holding up her hand. "Our lives will be different. There is no way around it. Joe barely squeaked past a high school diploma, and . . . well, he's poor. That means that likely he and I will always be poor. Hank is a doctor and was born wealthy. You may work, sis, but you won't have to. Your life will be a stark contrast to the one you were born into."

Amberley moved to sit beside her sister. "What are you trying to say?"

Brenda folded her hands in her lap and looked into Amberley's eyes. "What I am saying is that we have both chosen our paths. I love Joe with all my heart, and I know you love Hank. The other things we can't help. I just wanted you to know that I will always love you as my dear sister and that I never want there to be a shadow between us, wherever our paths may take us. As we move from being young women to older women, I want you to know that I shall never be envious of you, but I will always thank the Lord that He has blessed you. I pray that you may never know poverty again in all your days."

Amberley put her arm around her sister and pulled her close. She had no proper response. Everything Brenda had said was true. If she and Hank married, they would be rich. Some would always suspect that she had been attracted to Hank's money, and she would never be able to convince them otherwise. Amberley knew in her heart of hearts that she did not seek wealth. She had carefully followed God's leading, and He had allowed her to fall in love with a weary medical student, not for what he could do for her but for what she could do for him.

Releasing Brenda from her tight embrace, Amberley

smiled and said, "Brenda, all that you say is true. I'm not going to dig myself into a hole by trying to match your eloquence. I love you and we will always be sisters, and if I have anything to do with it, you and Joe and Hank and I will always be a family—a close family." Brenda looked at her sister and smiled. Amberley lowered her head and then, looking up at her sister again, said, "Yeah, I know. I'm just a goody-goody."

Brenda grinned a big grin and gave her sister a squeeze as she recalled the insult she had once hurled at Amberley when they were young girls.

"Now," Amberley said. "No more of this! Let's finish getting ready and go downstairs. If I am right, our guests should be here in time for a late breakfast or an early lunch."

* * *

Hank sat along the wall of glass windows, watching the planes land at the airport in South Bend. His father and mother were due in from Chicago within the half-hour, and he constantly checked his watch. Hank had rented a limousine at his father's request to accommodate their baggage and all of the presents they had brought. Hank smiled to think that his father, Craig Wheeler, Esquire, should have taken such a change. According to his mother, he had thoroughly enjoyed himself Christmas shopping.

Hank was happy that his parents were coming to spend Christmas, which also showed their willingness to accept Amberley. The thing that was still a mystery was whether or not his brother Richard would show up from California. Hank had spoken to Mai Lee the night before, and even though they had purchased plane tickets, she was not sure that Richard would come. The deep waters of bitterness flowed there, and Richard was not prepared to forgive his father for the way he had treated his wife and children.

They would know soon enough. Richard's plane, if he did indeed come, was due in about the same time as his father's.

Twenty-Four
Christmas on the Big Farm

 Christmas morning came with a quiet hush. The gray, overcast skies and occasional lake-effect snow showers from Lake Michigan alternated with intervals of blue sky and sunshine. It seemed that Christmas Day took an eternity to arrive, but once there, sought to escape in an instant like a thief through a window. The day was to be enjoyed and savored, moment by moment, as it would soon slip away until the next year.
 Richard, his wife Mai Lee, and the twins did indeed come. It seemed that Richard's desire to heal the rift with his father had overcome his harbored feelings of resentment. An emotional reunion at the airport and a sincere apology to an outcast daughter-in-law cleared the way to an enjoyable holiday. The twins in their innocence, not knowing of their grandfather's former feelings of disdain toward them, hugged him close and melted his heart.
 Breakfast that morning was light and happy as everyone crowded around the big table. Lien and the twins ate at

a card table in the corner, and she was pleasantly surprised that their mother had taught them to speak Vietnamese. Lien looked forward to spending time later with Mai Lee and talking about the old country. She was very beautiful and educated, and it was obvious that she had come from an important family in Saigon.

Craig Wheeler seemed to be infatuated with Sam. He wanted to get to know this man whom Lien so revered, and whom she said reminded her of himself. They spoke together of the farm and Sodus and some of Sam's exploits in the Special Forces. Sam avoided speaking of those days unless prodded and was surprised that Craig Wheeler was a knowledgeable fan of the Green Berets. As they chatted, Mary and Grandma Andrews made Marjorie Wheeler feel at home. They soon found that she was just "plain folk"—if she was haughty and high society, she didn't seem to know it of herself!

Soon breakfast was over, and everyone repaired to the large living room to open presents. It seemed that the Wheelers had gone overboard in their shopping, and the walls and area around the Christmas tree were stacked high with their gifts. All too soon it was afternoon and dinnertime, with turkey and dressing, mashed potatoes and gravy, cornbread-and-onion stuffing, pies and cakes and plenty of hot coffee. It was hard to perceive that Craig Wheeler was an austere Chicago attorney, feared by all and loved by none, as he happily played with his grandchildren on the floor in front of the tree.

***

Late afternoon came, and darkness would soon be upon the big farm in Sodus Township. Sam had harnessed up Gray and taken Mr. Wheeler on a sleigh ride through Hipps Hollow to the river. Mary, Grandma Andrews, Marjorie Wheeler, and Mrs. Schenkle sat on either side of the fireplace and talked over a pot of freshly brewed tea. Brenda and Joe, Karl and Beth, and Amberley and Hank sat on the long couch and chatted. Mai Lee and Lien sat together on the leather settee in the corner next to the Christmas tree, trying to remember a country and a former life that no longer existed. Lien found that her new friend was able to comfort her about her parents by expressing her own sorrow at leaving Vietnam forever. They softly wept together, and Mai Lee promised to write her often, giving her an opportunity to correspond with someone in the language of her birth.

It was getting late, and Karl knew that he still had responsibilities to the farm. As he stood up to put on his hat and coat, Grandma Andrews spoke up. "Karl, before you go, don't you think you should finish opening all of your presents?"

The look on Karl's face showed that he did not understand.

"There is still something under the tree for you," Grandma Andrews said.

Karl bent down, and sure enough, there was a manila envelope stuffed back under the tree against the wall. Karl got on his hands and knees, reached in, and pulled it out. The envelope was old and worn and soiled with finger smudges. "I don't get it," Karl said, looking at Mary and Grandma Andrews, who were smiling back at him. Karl turned the envelope over, and there, written in pencil with a scrawling hand, were the words: "To Karl and Beth from Jeb."

Surprised, Karl carefully opened the envelope, pulling out a stack of papers. As he read through them, his mouth dropped open, and he handed them to Beth to read.

"He wanted you two to have it," Grandma Andrews said with tears in her eyes. "It was his inheritance."

Beth read the papers and then looked up at Karl with glistening eyes. "Jeb has given us the deed to his sixty acres of land. We have a farm! Bless that dear, sweet old man!"

Grandma Andrews stood up and put her arms around Karl and Beth. "Jeb loved you both and wanted you to be happy. He somehow knew that he wasn't long for this world, and he asked me to transfer the deed to your names and give it to you now so you would have a place to build your home and raise a family."

Karl and Beth sat down next to each other on the long couch and held hands. What a year this had been in their lives, and the lives of everyone there! God had been kind to them all, and that truth had became most clear on this day: the day set aside to honor and celebrate the birth of His Son, the Lord Jesus Christ.

Twenty-Five
Surely Unexpected

Sam stood silently in the barnyard, gazing at the reddish sky to the west. It was dusk, and the air was beginning to chill. He could hear the uneasy sounds of the chickens as they settled on their roosts. It was early springtime, and whatever heat the sun had garnered that day quickly vanished as the shadows lengthened. He had just bid Karl good night and was returning to the house with a basket of brown eggs when, coming up the long driveway, he could see a pair of headlights. As they came near, he could see that it was a new pickup truck, fire-engine red. The truck parked near the back steps. When the doors opened, there were Amberley and Brenda.

"Hi, Daddy!" the girls shouted in unison.

"Well, I'll be . . . I didn't expect to see you girls this weekend. I thought you were spending it with college friends. Whose truck is this?"

"It's Hank's, Daddy. He bought it for us to use. He doesn't want us wearing out the Studebaker, and he said we will just ruin it by driving it back and forth."

Sam shook his head, amused and consternated at the same time. Hank was wealthy and that was obvious, but Sam was not going to argue with his display of chivalry. He agreed that it would be a shame to wear out the fine old car that Mrs. Holloway had restored for the girls. Besides, he didn't want to deny such a practical benefit to his two daughters. "Well, c'mon inside. Have you eaten your supper?"

"Yes, sir," Amberley answered.

Sam walked through the kitchen door and set the eggs on the table. "Look what followed me in, ladies," Sam said as Mary and Grandma Andrews looked up.

"Girls! We didn't expect to see you!" Mary exclaimed. "Is anything wrong?"

"No, Ma," Brenda answered. "We changed our plans and decided to come home."

"Have you had your supper? Are you girls eating enough?"

"We're just fine, Ma. Really we are," Brenda said, standing next to her sister with their backs to the stove.

Sam sat down next to Mary and took a raisin scone off the plate to dunk in his coffee. "Mary, it looks like Karl and Beth are finally settling in," he said with a chuckle. "It's hard to believe that just a year ago, Karl came to us out of nowhere, and now he is married and living in Jeb's old cabin."

"I know. They are such a sweet couple," Mary said. "I wish they would have taken our offer and come to live with us in the house, but I suppose they need their privacy. It will be sometime before they have a proper house to live in . . . girls! Are you whispering secrets?"

Amberley and Brenda were standing in the corner, whispering into each other's ears.

Mary frowned. "You know how I feel about that. It's rude, and I know I've taught you better."

"But Ma—" Amberley tried to speak.

"No buts! I declare! Has college so eroded your manners? You would think you girls to be silly teenagers, still in grade school and . . ."

Mary couldn't finish her sentence. Speechless, she put her hand to her mouth and stood up. Amberley and Brenda both beamed smiles as they held up their left hands. There in the glow of the kitchen light sparkled two engagement rings.

"Oh, girls! Are you sure this is wise? What about college?" Mary blurted out, still in shock.

"We're only officially engaged, Ma," Brenda explained. "There will be plenty of time to finish college."

Mary held the girls' hands. Amberley's ring was a beautiful polished gold, with a large diamond and several smaller stones on each side. It looked enormous on her petite hand and had a wonderful, warm fire. Brenda's ring barely gave off a faint glint of light, for it was only silver with a very small stone and diamond chips. Mary looked into Brenda's eyes as if she could read her daughter's thoughts. They were beginning to well up with tears.

"I know, Ma, I know," she whispered. "It took everything that Joe had to buy it. But he is as proud of it as if it were the crown jewels of England. And it is, Ma! To me it really is!"

Mary hugged her daughters and kissed them both.

"Well, this was surely unexpected," Sam said, standing up to kiss his girls too. "I guess it was bound to happen sooner or later, and I can't think of two finer men than Joe and Hank."

Standing in the corner, thin and silent, was Lien. Amberley noticed her standing there, looking small and alone and unwilling to accept that her world was changing, and she hurried to embrace her.

"Oh, honey, please don't be sad," she whispered softly. "You knew this was probably going to happen. And you like Joe and Hank, don't you?"

"Yes," Lien said, still looking at the floor.

"Don't you want us to be happy?"

"Yes, Amber. I just don't want you to go away. I will be all alone."

"You will see us a whole lot. This will always be our home. Please don't be sad. I couldn't get married if you were not happy for me!"

"Neither could I," said Brenda.

Lien smiled and lifted her head. Her eyes were sparkling. "I *am* very happy for you, and I like Joe and Hank very much."

"All right then," Amberley said, "and just remember, someday soon you will find a beau of your own and get married. And we will all like him just fine!"

* * *

Sam and Mary sat at the kitchen table, holding each other's hands. It was late, and everyone had long gone up to bed. Finally, with a yawn and a stretch, Sam stood up, set his coffee cup in the sink, and checked the lock on the kitchen door. Putting his arm around his wife, he walked up the stairs by her side. Pausing on the top step, Sam looked into Mary's eyes.

"Weren't Amberley and Brenda just little girls a while ago?" he asked.

"Yes, Sam," Mary answered, kissing him on the cheek. "I think it was just yesterday."

THE END

CPSIA information can be obtained
at www.ICGtesting.com
Printed in the USA
FFOW01n0339280915
17244FF